TEXAS DADDY

WISHBONE TEXAS

ANN B HARRISON

TEXAS DADDY

TEXAS DADDY

Texas Daddy
Wishbone Texas #5
Copyright2024 Ann B Harrison
All rights reserved.

This is a book of fiction. Names, characters, places, brands, media and incidents are either the product of the authors imagination or are used fictitiously. The author acknowledges the trademark status and trademark owners of various products referred to in this work of fiction, which have been used without permission. The publication/use of these trademarks is not authorized, associated with, or sponsored by the trademark owners.

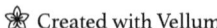 Created with Vellum

1

Cassie crouched down on the pavement, so she was at eye level with Daniel. Her heart beating savagely in her chest and once again she questioned the rash decision to steal this child from his mother and run.

She hadn't given much thought to how this would destroy her career or upset the people around her, including the ones that relied on her at the women's shelter, but it was something she couldn't take back. Nor would she if she was given the option. There hadn't been time to think, only to act. It was a life or death decision; act now or stay and they both die. She didn't have the luxury of weighing up the impact of her choice.

"Daniel, you have to be real good now, you hear me? Just hold my hand and say nothing. Let me do the talking."

He looked at her with wide blue, fear filled eyes. For someone so young, he was one of the most resilient kids she'd met. "But I just want my daddy." His eyes turned glassy and his lip quivered as he held his stuffed teddy to his chest.

She pulled him close, rubbing circles on his back to calm him down. Her own nerves were frayed but Daniel came first. She could have her meltdown later once she knew he was safe. "I know you do, buddy but we have to do it this way, okay? It's for the best."

The best for her that was. If she drove up to the ranch with Daniel right now, all hell would break loose. She needed someone to guide her in and keep the family calm. It was her best chance at not being arrested for kidnapping. On top of everything that had happened, that wasn't what she needed.

"Your Aunt Ella can call Daddy for you and then we will go to the ranch and see him, okay?"

Daniel sniffed as he nodded.

Cassie stood and grabbed his hand, staring at the shop window decorated with fourth of July merchandise. No matter how Ella treated her when they walked in the door, Cassie had to admit she had a way with color and style. A small slither of envy poked up its head before she pushed it down. Cassie sucked in a fortifying breath. Her career took all of her time and the last thing she was going to do was ditch that for a life of decorating. Unless she got fired for her actions. "Let's go."

She strode toward the door and opened it, giving Daniel a quick glance as she guided him inside, smiling to alleviate his fears.

"Welcome to Ella's homewares. Holler out if we can help you at all."

Cassie stared at the woman speaking to them from behind the counter and her heart dropped. It wasn't Ella Wilson. She wasn't expecting someone else to be in the store.

"Um, hi. Thank you but I was wondering if I could speak to Ella." She stepped toward the counter, her palms sweaty.

The young blonde lady waved a hand, as if dismissing her comment. "Nope. Sorry. Ella is on maternity leave. Can I help you at all?"

Sweat beaded on Cassie's lip and noise rang in her ears. She'd been so tense coming into this little Texas town and being stumped at the first post had thrown her more than she expected. *What am I going to do? Ella was the only lifeline to this part of her plan.* Backup wasn't something she even had time to contemplate.

The woman stepped from behind the counter and came to her with a frown on her face. "Darlin' are you okay? You've gone mighty pale." She grabbed Cassie's arm and pulled her over to a small settee, pushing her down.

"Put your head down between your knees before you pass out."

Cassie felt her head being pushed down and didn't protest. She was struggling to not lose consciousness.

"Do you want me to call a family member for you, maybe your husband?"

Cassie shook her head. That was the last thing she needed.

"How about I get an ambulance for you?"

Cassie pushed herself to her feet, putting out a hand when her world spun. She swallowed and blinked a few times to try and regain her composure. "No thank you. I'll be fine."

The woman wasn't to be put off. "You sure don't look fine to me, and your boy here looks terrified. Are you sure I can't do something to help you?"

"No, we'll be fine." She reached for Daniel's hand, but he stepped away from her, terror in his eyes.

"How about you sit down for a minute and gather your wits before you go running off." She held onto Cassie's arm gently. "My name is Sienna and I work for Ella. I can give her a call if you like." She pressed Cassie back down onto the settee.

"I'm going to get you both a cold drink before you go anywhere. Just sit and don't move, okay?" She raced off before waiting for an answer.

Cassie glanced at Daniel, trying to soften her features by smiling at him. He pressed his back into the counter Sienna had been standing behind when they arrived. "Daniel, it's okay. I just had a moment, okay. I'm fine honey. I didn't mean to scare you."

He stood with his fingers in his mouth, the dirty toy collecting dribble, watching her but not coming any closer. He was scared, she knew enough about his history to understand exactly what was going through his little head. The amount of times he'd seen his mother stoned out of her mind had left an impression on him and her having a moment like this had only reminded him of that.

"We'll be fine, sweetheart. I promise you that."

"Here we are, young man. A glass of water for you and a popsicle and a nice cold water for your momma."

Daniel glanced at Cassie, a question in his eyes.

"Take it, sweetheart. I think we both need a cold drink. It was getting a little hot outside. It's probably what made me feel a little funny." Her heart still beat wildly in her chest, but she did her best not to let it show. It was easy to blame the warm weather for her incident rather than allow Daniel or Sienna to know it was a full-on panic attack. She smiled as she took the glass offered to her. "Thank you so much. Sorry to be such a bother. I don't know why the heat suddenly got to me like that. Must have been a bit dehydrated."

"Y'all sit and take your time. I'm not busy and it's nice to see a new face in town. So, you're a friend of Ella's?"

Cassie held the cool glass between her hands and took a steadying breath. "Not really a friend as such. We met once and got on real well. I thought I'd pop in and say hello since we're in town."

Sienna smiled and glanced around the shop. "Well, I can tell her you called in but she won't be back at work for at least another few weeks. Her and Travis are both taking time off so they can bond as a family." She closed her eyes and smiled dreamily. "The bliss of a new baby." Then she laughed and turned to Daniel.

"How are you now, young man? Feeling a bit better?"

He nodded and dropped his head so Cassie couldn't see his eyes, but his body had begun to tremble. She should have known that another stranger was enough to trigger his anxiety. What if he broke down and she couldn't explain it away? They needed to get out of here before he said something he shouldn't. Cassie downed the water and handed the glass back to Sienna. "Thank you. I really needed that. I'm feeling much better now." She stood and reached for Daniel's hand, noticing the business cards on the counter. One for the shop, another for a lawyer and one for the coffee shop down the street with a bonus free coffee offer. She could do with a caffeine hit.

She quickly grabbed one of each, keeping the coffee card on the top. "I'll check out the website and maybe catch up with Ella another time." She turned toward the door. "I appreciate your help. You have a nice day now."

Cassie couldn't get out of the shop fast enough. When the door shut behind them, she let out a sigh of relief. She didn't let go of Daniel's hand until they were in the car. Only then did she bother to read the cards she'd grabbed.

Fifth coffee free! The address of the coffee shop was just down the street and she resisted the urge to head there. She slipped that card to the bottom and read the next one, more to give her time to settle than anything else.

Small family law firm.

The card was plain, almost boring in its design. No flashy fonts or wild promises. *Confidentiality guaranteed!*

Was this a sign?

Maybe, just maybe she needed more than a soft introduction to the family. Perhaps it would be in her best interest to do this with someone watching her back instead of her being the protector.

She read the details and put the address into her phone. It was only a few minutes away. If Ella wasn't available to ease her footsteps to the ranch, she might be well advised to seek legal advice.

***

A man glanced up from his computer as she opened the front door. He stared and smiled as if to say – 'At last, a customer.'

Cassie felt a tremor of apprehension roll down her back as he stood with the confidence and eagerness of a man ready to work his charm.

He walked towards them, a welcoming smile on his face. "Hello. Come on in. How can I help you?"

"I don't know if you can."

He guided her to a chair. "Let me be the judge of that." He pointed to a child's desk in the corner of the room with coloring in pencils and a handful of books. "Perhaps the young guy would like to entertain himself while we talk?"

"Good idea. It's okay Daniel. I'm just here." She watched

him take a seat and when he picked up a colored pencil and started drawing, she sucked in a fortifying breath, not waiting for him to give a formal introduction in case she lost her nerve. In a whispered voice, careful not to be overheard by Daniel, Cassie filled him in on the bare basics of the story.

By the time she was finished, the lawyer was in a panic. His face had paled, and a stunned expression came over him. He sat back in his chair, eyes wide and his mouth open. It took a couple of minutes for him to gather himself and get out the words.

"That's my nephew? Daniel, is it really you?" He got up from his chair and moved around the desk, crouching down next to the frightened child. "Hey buddy, you won't remember me but I'm your Uncle Eli."

"No." Cassie moaned and swayed in her seat, her fingers digging into the cushion. "It can't be."

He stared at her, as if he were torn between helping her and hugging his nephew. "I thought you came to me because you saw my name on that card you have. You did, didn't you?"

She put her head in her hands and shook her head.

"Okay, I'll take that as a no then."

"I can't believe I was so stupid not to put two and two together. Eli Wilson, Adam Wilson. What are the odds of you being brothers?"

Eli stood and shrugged. "Small town, makes sense, doesn't it?"

"I'm screwed, aren't I?"

Eli propped his hip on the corner of the desk. "How do you mean?"

"You'll call the sheriff and hand me in. Technically I kidnapped Daniel."

Eli stared at the little boy, a flash of wonder in his eyes. Cassie wondering how he was going to do this. He was likely desperate to call Adam and tell him Daniel was safe and she didn't blame him. She'd do the exact same in his place.

"We could argue that point and technically, you're my client and anything you tell me is privileged information. I can't turn you in."

She all but collapsed in her chair with relief. He walked around the desk and took a seat, his gaze constantly going back to his nephew.

"I can advise you, but I can't force you to do anything. But you came to bring Daniel home, right?"

She nodded.

"I would advise you to take him home to his father then. Adam has been beside himself ever since Daniel was taken."

It was something she could understand. It wasn't often she witnessed the suffering of the fathers in her job at the shelter, it was usually the distraught or desperate woman she was helping care for as a phycologist, women running from a bad relationship or who find themselves homeless with no way of feeding their children but the suffering is often the same when it comes to the loss of a child due to a custody issue. "I understand and that's why I'm here. The reason I went to Ella's shop was to get someone to help me ease into this. I didn't want to just front up and say, hey I stole your son from your ex. You can have him back now." She smiled sadly at Daniel. This had probably cost her way more than she could imagine and even though she understood Adam would be furious as well as grateful. Either way could be bad news for Cassie.

Eli leaned forward on his desk. "I can't do anything you don't want me to do. Okay? I can advise you, but I can't call my brother and tell him you're here unless you instruct me to."

"Why not?"

"You're my client now. I can't break that confidentiality." He chewed on his bottom lip. "Not unless you die, or we get dragged through court."

She paled again and Eli seemed to regret his words, but she was in for a heck of a grilling from more the rest of the family, and she knew it. Bringing Daniel home may have been a split-second decision, but she had considered the consequences of her actions the entire anxious drive here. And there was more than she had even started to process, but the first of those consequences would be facing Adam and his family.

He gave her a gentle smile. "Why don't I call Mama and tell her someone is calling in, so she is kind of prepared and she can call Adam up to the house. Once I know you're at the ranch, I can come out and be your support person."

She was going to need one and she knew it. His family was pretty full on according to Lissa, Daniel's mom and there was a heap of them which could be overwhelming if you weren't used to it. Being an only child, she had never had to deal with a big family.

"Why can't you come with me?" She clutched her hands together.

"Okay, so this is where I speak to you as your lawyer and not Daniel's uncle. I feel the best choice for you in this situation is for you to be seen as making this choice to go to the ranch under your own volition and without any persuasion or influence by me. I want the law to see you as being proactive, not forced to hand Daniel over. If for any reason this handover is discussed in court or a legal setting – and I'm not saying it will be – it may make a difference, but you're right – you kidnapped him regardless of why.

"If you think that's what's best." She gave him a quick smile and then sighed, wondering if she had done the right thing coming here. She had been through hell since she snatched Daniel. She was exhausted; physically, mentally and emotionally. All she needed was to get this boy home safely and find somewhere to lay her head down and sleep for a week. Then she would decide what her next move would be.

"I do." His eyes softened slightly, "No matter what happens, you have me now, okay? I'll take care of anything and everything I can. You may get arrested, so be prepared for that."

She stiffened and inhaled a sharp breath. Of course she had known this was a real possibility, probability even. But hearing it from Eli made the threat seem even more real.

She bowed her head and Daniel ran over and wrapped his arms around her waist, his head in her lap as he began to cry.

Eli frowned as if the words had been a wrong choice he couldn't take back. "Hey, Daniel, buddy. It's going to be okay. I'll look after Cassie, I promise. But your Daddy is waiting for you at home so maybe it's time he got to see you."

He wrote the address of the ranch on a slip of paper and pushed it across the desk. "I'll give you ten minutes head start, then I'll be right behind you, okay?"

"Sure. I may as well get this done with."

"Give me five seconds. You need to sign a client agreement." He clicked the mouse and chose a file, sending it to the printer. Once it churned out the pages, he grabbed them and passed them over the desk with a pen for her signature.

Cassie signed it without hesitation. Eli Wilson seems

like her best chance of getting Daniel home and her avoiding prison...hopefully. She sighed and placed the pen down. "No matter what happens to me, I'm happy knowing that Daniel has been returned to his father where he belongs. If I end up in jail, it'll be worth it. I couldn't leave him with her any longer. I just couldn't, not in those circumstances." Her lungs constricted making it hard for her to breathe and she pressed a hand to her chest.

Eli frowned and sadness swept over his face as if he'd just realized exactly how much she had given up to be at this point. "You're a good woman, Cassie and I thank you from the bottom of my heart. I will look after you, I promise."

2

Cassie pulled up at the front of the house just as the door opened and a woman came bustling out, wiping her hands on her apron. She had a wary smile on her face as she approached the car.

Cassie opened the door and stepped out, holding open the back door for Daniel as he fumbled with his seat belt.

"Do I know you, sugar?" She squinted at Cassie, shielding her eyes from the sun.

"No ma'am, but I believe you know this little guy in the back seat."

Daniel climbed out and the woman let out a gasp, her hand coming up to cover her heart before she screamed, rushing to Daniel, only pausing when Daniel backed into Cassie for protection.

An elderly man came running out of the house. "What the heck...."

"Daddy, our boy is home. Daniel is here." Tears streaked down the woman's face.

"Daniel? Really?" The old man hobbled over to the car and stared at the child. "Daniel?"

"It's him, it's really him." The woman crouched down and started stroking the child's face. "Do you remember me, Daniel?"

Daniel's bottom lip trembled, as he let out a whimper and pulled away from her, hiding around the back of Cassie's legs.

"It's been a long trip, and he's scared." She hugged Daniel and he climbed up on her hip, wrapping his arms around her neck tight enough to almost choke her. His tiny body shook as he buried his face into her neck.

"Oh my lord, it really is him." The elderly gentleman turned and ran down the side of the house calling for Adam.

"I'm sorry, sugar. I didn't mean to scare him. I'm Babs, Daniel's Grandma." She wiped her eyes with her apron. "Come inside, both of you. This is such a huge occasion, and I'm flustered. Please, come in and have coffee. Adam will be up as soon as Grandpa can find him."

"Nice to meet you. My name is Cassie. Cassie Sanders." Daniel tucked his face into Cassie's neck. "Grandpa." His little voice was barely audible.

The woman turned, a delighted smile on her face. "That's right, sugar. You remember Grandpa?"

She put a hand on Cassie's arm. "Call me Babs, sugar. You can tell me all about how you come to have Daniel with you when we get you settled. Oh, my word, I don't believe this. Our little man is finally home."

She opened the door and ushered Cassie inside a large entry and pushed her toward the kitchen. "In here, sugar."

Cassie stood with the child in her arms looking around the huge home. It looked like something out of a designer magazine.

"Have a seat." Babs poured her a coffee at the large breakfast bar and opened a container of cookies and pushed them toward her. "These were your favorites, Daniel."

Daniel turned his head enough to look at them before he reached out and took one. He took a bite and snuggled back into Cassie's neck again.

"He's been through a lot."

Babs stood watching them, tears in her eyes. "I bet he has, poor child. What that woman must have put him through." She took a deep breath, before smiling at Cassie. "The story will come out and preferably when he's sleeping if you don't mind. You can tell us everything later. We've waited this long for him, the story isn't that important. What's important is that he is home, thanks to you." Fresh tears filled her eyes, and she cleared her throat, "In the meantime, sit down and have a drink. You look totally exhausted, child." She was exhausted, to her very bones. It's lucky Daniel had such a tight grip on her, she wasn't sure her tired arms could actually hold him by herself.

Cassie propped herself up on the chair and started to slide Daniel on the one next to her when the back door burst open, and a man lurched into the room.

"Daniel?"

Daniel screamed and clambered back onto her lap, his little arms clutched Cassie around the neck even tighter than before and started wailing.

Adam stood staring at him, his face pale as a tidal wave of emotions crossed his handsome face; shock, relief, affection, but anger also flashed in his eyes. That she could understand after what he'd been through.

So long as he didn't take it out on her, Cassie could deal with it. She was too tired to care that much but after her visit to Eli, she knew anything could happen.

"I'm sorry, he's frightened and probably overwhelmed."

She soothed the child, stroking gentle circles on his back and hugging him to her as Adam continued to stare at her.

"Adam, sit down and stop scaring the boy. And wipe that thunderous look off your face too, sugar."

Adam blinked, as if coming out of a trance and then shifted his gaze to his mother.

She gave him a sympathetic glance and pointed at the chair furthest from Cassie and Daniel. "Sit." She poured him a coffee and slid it over the counter. "It's been a long time for this child, Adam. You're scaring him to death. Sit and be quiet and let him relax a little. He'll come around when he's good and ready."

Adam shook his head, refusing to sit. "No. Mama, I need answers. I need to hug my son, and I want to know why this woman has him!" His angry glare snapped back to Cassie, and she stiffened.

The front door closed, and footsteps came toward the kitchen. "You'll get all the answers you need, brother, once things calm down. Now do as Mama said and sit your butt in that chair and shut your mouth for five minutes." Eli stopped near Cassie and put a hand on her shoulder. Eli's reassuring touch on her shoulder prevented Cassie from shrinking under Adam's intimidating glare, but it didn't stop her heart from racing in her chest.

***.

Adam didn't take his eyes off his brother and the woman holding his son.

His son!

All the time Daniel had been missing, he'd prayed and hoped for this to happen and now it had, there were so many questions he wanted to ask. But his child was staring at him with huge, terrified eyes and it broke something inside of him.

Now anger burned up his throat. Who was this woman, why did she have his son when his ex-wife Lissa was the one who took him? And why was his brother protecting her?

Adam pointed a shaking finger at Cassie.

"If she's responsible for taking Daniel, I want her charged. Do you hear me, Eli. Call Clay and get him out here." He couldn't stop the tremor in his voice, no matter how much he tried.

"He's on his way." Eli stared him down.

Cassie gasped. "You called the sheriff on me? Why? How could you do that after all Daniel and I went through to get here?"

Daniel started to cry in her arms and Adam couldn't even console him. It was her fault. His son should be in his arms, not some strangers.

Eli held his hands up. "Calm down, Cassie. I called him because I know what kind of temper my brother has, and I was trying to protect you. He's not going to arrest you. You've done nothing wrong."

WTF? "Don't I have a right to be angry? My son was stolen from me. Stolen! You have no idea what the feels like." He couldn't control the rising of his voice no matter how much he tried.

Eli sighed and Adam knew there was a lecture coming his way. "You're right. I have no idea how that feels. But I do know this, Adam. That child is a mess right now and the only one who can calm him down and make him feel safe is Cassie. How about you and I walk outside and talk so he doesn't feel afraid. I think he's had enough of that these last few years, don't you?"

And just like that, Adam's anger deflated, and his heart fell to his stomach. How could he be so stupid? Of course, Daniel was going to be scared. It was obvious he no longer knew his own family. The poor boy was only a toddler when his mother took him. Goodness knows what his life had been like and here he was, scaring the crap out of him. *Way to welcome him home, Adam!*

Adam stared at him for a moment longer, feeling as if he needed to get all the memories he could in case he was taken away from him again before nodding. "Yeah." His eyes flickered to Cassie as she cradled his son against her chest, his face pressed to her neck as she whispered soft words into his ear. He clenched his jaw and stormed from the kitchen.

He stood with his hands on his hips, staring across the pasture with the mares and foals in it, waiting for his brother to come and tear a strip off him for being so stupid.

The screen door slammed moments before a hand landed on his shoulder. "Adam."

He couldn't help it, tears filled his eyes and his throat closed over. He'd been waiting for this for almost three years. Daniel was finally home, and he had no idea how to process it, how to deal with what he was feeling, nothing was going right.

He cleared his throat as Eli wrapped him in a big brotherly hug, patting his back as if he was a small child, just like he used to do when they were boys.

That opened up the floodgate and years of pain and anxiety seeped out of his body in a flood of tears. They stood like that until footsteps sounded on the gravel and Adam broke away, wiping his eyes with his sleeve.

His father and Grandpa stopped in front of them, worry on their faces. "Son, what's happened? Grandpa said a lady brought Daniel home."

Eli patted Adam on the arm giving him time to compose himself and spoke. "She's inside with him but Dad, take it easy. Poor kid is scared witless, and I can hardly blame him.

He barely remembers any of us. Cassie is the only thing he knows right now so we need to be mindful of that and not let our emotions overrun common sense."

His father stared at the kitchen window, swallowing a couple of times before speaking. "Who exactly is this, Cassie?"

"She has to tell that story, not me. If you give her a chance, she will clear everything up, but Mama said not in front of Daniel, and I agree. It's not a pretty story and the last thing a child needs to hear. We might have to wait for him to have a nap to get the whole story." Adam tensed under his hand.

"But you know it all, right?"

Eli stared his brother in the eyes. "Not everything but enough."

Adam couldn't help the sneer that curled his lip. "And you're still going to protect her?"

"You would too if you knew what I knew, brother. I know enough to stand by her and be eternally grateful for what she's been through to get here."

A car skidded into the driveway and Clay slowed as he came to them. Pushing open the door before he stopped, he jumped out. "Eli, tell me it's true." He strode over to them, his eyes glued to their brother.

Eli held up his hands. "Yes, it's true but as I was just saying to Dad here, you gotta slow down. Kid is terrified of us all right now. He only knows Cassie."

Clay leaned into Eli's face and pointed a finger at him. "Just who the heck is this, Cassie woman and why does she have him, not his mother?"

Adam could see that Eli was losing patience, but he didn't care. He had a right to know as much as anyone, more if the truth be told. It was his son.

Eli gave Clay a droll glance. "Cassie is the woman who brought Daniel home. That's all you need to concern yourself with right now. She will tell you the story when Daniel is asleep or otherwise distracted. No tough man stuff around the boy, understood?"

Clay shook his head. "No. You don't get to make the rules here Eli. You can smart mouth me all you want and defend her in court, if necessary, but that child was stolen from his father and now some woman fronts up with him and we don't get to ask questions until you say so? No way. I'm the sheriff here, I get to say what happens." He turned on his heel and walked into the house.

"Shit." Eli chased him.

Adam stood shellshocked and stared at their backs, wanting desperately to go inside as well but terrified he would upset his son again.

3

Cassie gripped Daniel tighter as the sheriff stormed into the kitchen. She kept her gaze on him as he quickly assessed the situation, seemingly ignoring Babs's warning look.

"Cassie, I assume? Do you have a surname?"

"Cassie Sanders and you are?" She lifted her chin a fraction. Two could play this game.

Eli butted in. "Clay, she's done nothing wrong. Stop acting like she's the bad guy here."

Babs walked around and stood beside Cassie, putting a hand on her back which felt incredibly like the kind of support she needed. Getting this far had been traumatic for both her and Daniel and she was so close to breaking point, it scared her witless. But before she broke, she had to make sure Daniel was okay.

"Clay Wilson, Wishbone Creeks Sheriff." He tipped his head to the window where the men stood staring in uncertainly as if scared to come in and get involved. "Adam is my brother, and that young man is my nephew."

Daniel huddled against her, a cookie in his hand forgotten as he stared at the stranger.

"Pleased to meet you, Sheriff."

"Would you care to fill me in on how come you have my nephew?"

Babs squeezed her shoulder, and Cassie took that as support.

"Not at this time. We've decided it would be best to wait until Daniel is asleep. He's suffered enough trauma already and as a child psychologist, it is my opinion that this conversation isn't something he needs to be involved in." She stared at him, watching the flicker in his eyes when she mentioned her profession.

Had he thought she was just some brainless female who happened to be involved with Daniel's mother?

"Psychologist?" He stared over her head at his mother. "Mama, what do you know about this?"

Babs stood straighter. "As Cassie says, we'll discuss this later when things calm down. Now, y'all can come and have a civilized cup of coffee and get to know Daniel quietly or go about your business and call back later when the child is sleeping. Your choice." She bustled back around the kitchen island, confident her word was law and Cassie was almost one hundred percent sure it was.

Clay stood staring at her for a moment before sighing, his shoulders slumping in defeat. He gave her a quick smile and nodded at the chair down from hers. "Do you mind?"

Cassie shook her head, hanging onto Daniel as he watched his uncle warily.

"I'm sorry I frightened you, Daniel. It wasn't what I meant to do." He perched on the chair, removed his hat and reached for the coffee Babs slid across to him, "Thanks Mama".

He placed his hat on the counter and glanced at them, his face softer than it had been when he'd walked in. "How about we start over. Is that okay with you?" He smiled warmly and waited patiently for Daniel to reply.

"What do you say, Daniel? We talked about this, right?" Cassie felt the little body relax against her. "Good boy. I'm not going anywhere, ok. You're safe, no one here will hurt you, okay? Don't forget that."

He glanced up at her with a mix of fear and doubt in his eyes and it almost broke her heart. He'd been through so much in his few years on the planet and didn't deserve half of it. That's what made her throw caution to the wind and grab him when she did, ignoring what consequences she would suffer in the process.

Cassie smiled and dropped a kiss on his nose and Daniel laughed for the first time in ages, it was barely audible, but it was there. "That tickles." At the sound of his soft voice warmth bloomed in her chest.

The back door opened, and his father and the rest of the men walked silently into the room, pausing at the sound. Adam stared at her. So many emotions crossed his face, love, heartbreak, desperation, all as his eyes begged her for help, but she couldn't do anything for him. She was totally invested in Daniels well-being and that was where her focus would remain until this was over. The little boy in her arms was all that mattered.

Eli pushed past his family and walked around to his mother, wrapping her in a big hug, resting his chin on the top of her head. "Mama, I need coffee, a cookie and a promise from you."

He winked at Cassie.

"Promise? What is it this time, Eli?" She batted him away and poured a mug of coffee for him.

"I want you to make sure you look after Cassie for me. I need to head back to town shortly for a court session, but I will be back later." He sipped his coffee before glancing at the other men in the room before his gaze rested on Cassie. "If I hear so much as any one of you have given my client more than an encouraging or welcoming word, you will deal with me. Understood?" Cassie lifted her chin, her spine straight. She was determined to evoke confidence and bravery, even if she didn't feel it.

He glanced at them one by one, his gaze lingering on his brother Adam, Daniel's father.

Babs glanced at her and gave her a quick wink before answering Eli. "Ain't nobody going to hurt that girl, I can promise you that." Babs held her cheek up for a kiss and then gave him a push toward the door as he reached over and snatched a cookie. "Go. She'll be fine."

He gave her a small salute as he walked out the door and despite the protection from Babs, and the bravado she'd shown seconds earlier, Cassie felt her shoulders tense.

***.

Adam walked around the kitchen island to stand beside his mother. Not for protection but to get a better look at his son with the distance between them to discourage him from what he wanted to do most – grab Daniel and never let him go again.

He'd dreamed of this moment for the last three years and now it was here, he couldn't quite believe it. When Lissa hadn't returned him from an access visit, his heart had almost broken. For three long years they'd been searching for him with no luck. They never even knew if he was dead or alive.

Daniel had grown but not as much as Adam would have expected. Was his mother feeding him properly? Was she looking after him as much as he deserved? She'd shown that she was totally unreliable so many times, Adam didn't believe his son was her first priority.

He had shadows under his eyes and his skin was pale. He clutched the chocolate chip cookie as if he was scared it would be taken from him. His spindly little legs had scars and faded bruises. Not unusual in a child, but these weren't in places he would expect. Every child got skinned knees and bruises down the front of their legs from running into things but not on the side or the back of their calves. Small round bruises that could easily be from a strong hand or cigarette burn.

His stomach churned thinking about what Daniel had been through. It was his own fault, and he mentally kicked himself. He, more than anyone, knew that Lissa wasn't to be trusted but he'd allowed her to take him for a visit. How could he have been so stupid?

He swallowed and sipped the coffee his mother pushed into his hands, the bitterness coating the back of his throat.

"Have a cookie, Adam and stop worrying. Things will all turn out fine. Daniel is home and that's the only thing that matters."

His mom was right, he took a couple of cookies from the container she held in front of him.

"Daniel, would you like another one?" She pushed the container across toward the boy and he watched as Daniel's eyes widened and he glanced at Cassie for approval.

Cassie kissed the top of his head and smiled at him. "It's okay, buddy. You can have as many as you like." Her eyes filled with tears as she stroked his head, her gaze meeting Adams. When she talked to his son, her face softened. The sweet smiles she gave him soothed Daniel and lessened his anxiety. It was clear that the affection she felt for him was genuine and that pulled at Adam's heart. He was torn between berating her for having Daniel and thanking her for her kindness.

His heart pounded and he felt like the worst person in the world. She'd brought his son home. How she'd managed to get hold of him didn't matter. The fact that Daniel was here, and she'd been the one to return him should mean more than how she was involved. He caught her eye and mouthed a silent, "Thank you." He couldn't trust his voice. Her face softened, as she attempted to blink back her tears.

Adam leaned his elbows on the counter, his body sagging in relief. It was finally hitting home that his boy was back, and his knees felt weak like a newborn calf. His chest ached and his breath started to come in short pants. Hands grabbed at him, and he was pushed onto a stool.

Grandpa whispered in his ear. "You're okay, Adam. Just breath and thank God he's home safe. All the rest can wait until later."

His father patted him on the back as he cleared his throat, tears close. "I hope you intend staying for a while, Cassie. We started off on the wrong foot and I apologize for that. We'd like to have you stick around and I'm sure Daniel would like that too. Right, Daniel?"

His son nodded his head, a small smile lifting the corners of his mouth.

"Right, that's settled then." He wiped his hand across his face and smiled. "Guess we'd better get back to work, Grandpa, what do you say? Leave this young man and Cassie to settle in and we can see them later at dinner."

Grandpa nodded. "Yep, so much to do. Maybe if he feels up to it, Cassie could maybe bring him down to the barn for a little walk later. Only if he wants too though. Plenty of time to get back into the swing of things." He patted Daniel on the head gently. "Up to you, young man but if you feel up to a walk, we have some baby chickens down there." When Grandpa walked out of the kitchen, tears were rolling down his cheeks.

It's the first time Adam had ever seen his Grandpa cry.

4

Adam kept watching the road to the house, hoping that Daniel would want to come down and see the baby chickens. He used to love playing in the barn when he was a toddler. Before his mother stole him and ran.

Adam didn't want to leave Daniel, not even for a moment. The fear he would disappear again was a living, breathing thing, sitting on his chest. But his Mama had insisted he give Cassie and Daniel some space and she'd been right, he knew that. Cassie had looked ready to break. She'd also seemed ready to defend, like a lioness ready to rip anyone apart who dared threaten her cub. Her protectiveness was welcome, it worked as a balm for his frazzled nerves. He could leave Daniel knowing she was there to protect him. She *did* protect him...when he didn't.

"Stop worrying, son. He'll come down when he feels it's safe to do so. Poor kid probably has a lot to deal with right now and this is the best place for him. We both know that. Time fixes most things if you let it." His father slapped him on the back and kept walking.

Adam felt the lump in his throat. He knew his father was right but that didn't stop him feeling so desperate to hold his son again. Even though Daniel had eventually smiled at him in the kitchen, he still clung to Cassie. He knew he should feel grateful to her, but it was hard not to also feel jealous of the connection she had to his boy. Just what had she done to earn that, he wondered.

"Adam, got ourselves a lame horse. Checked her over and can't see what's wrong. Want me to call the vet?"

He turned and focused on the paint mare the cowboy had brought over, going over her body bit by bit, looking for anything that could have caused the lameness. "Was she out in the pasture with the other mares?"

Dean adjusted his hat before answering. "Yeah, was checking a new foal and noticed it. Thought we should check her out before it gets any worse." He patted the mare on the neck and leaned into her, whispering soothing words.

Adam smoothed his hand down her flank again and paused as she moved her feet. "I think she may have been kicked." He rubbed at a small dirty mark, feeling the muscles quiver under his touch. "Put her in the stable for now and see how she goes. Some of those mares get a little bit precious now and then. She's not due to foal for a couple of weeks and was probably just being nosy but I don't want to risk her or the foal getting hurt."

"You got it, boss." The cowboy led the mare away to an empty stable and walked her in, talking to her. Adam stood by as he filled her feed bin and gave her a scratch around the ears.

A movement near the barn door caught his eye and his breath caught in his throat. Cassie walked toward him with Daniel gripping her hand with both of his.

Cassie smiled and paused a few feet away. "Daniel wanted to show me the chickens. It seems he remembers coming down and helping with them."

Adam swallowed the emotion that threatened to choke him. His son remembered. He cleared his throat. "Well, we just so happen to have a little momma in the end stable with a clutch of chicks. She's been pretty protective and won't let anyone in there. Maybe Daniel could sweettalk her." He glanced at Cassie feeling as if he had to explain. "He always had a way with them."

"I'd love to see them. Daniel, do you want to show me?"

Daniel nodded, keeping close to her body.

"This way." Adam moved toward the stable where Grandpa had found the cranky momma chicken earlier in the week. As they stood at the door, she clucked and fluffed out her feathers as if to scare them.

Daniel gave a giggle and crouched down, still holding onto Cassie with one hand, reached out to the chicken wiggling his fingers.

The momma settled down and pecked at the hay around her, pulling it close to her body. A little head popped out from under her feathers and Daniel glanced up at Adam, his finger on his lips. "Shh."

Adam's heart just about burst. His son had turned to him. He blinked and risked a glance at Cassie. She was smiling at him as if she knew how much this meant to him.

Just breathe, Adam, you got this. Don't go scaring the poor boy.

5

By the time Cassie had fed, bathed and put Daniel to bed in some pyjamas that Babs had given her from her other grandson, she was sorely tempted to climb in beside him. Their afternoon had been bouts of excitement of discovering elements of the ranch he used to know, crossed with moments of fear that it would all disappear again, and she'd done her best to soothe Daniel as his mood fluctuated.

Refusing to sleep on his own had been the last shred of defiance before he finally conceded to sleep, and she was too tired to care. They'd shared a bed in the dingy motels they'd stayed at along the way, so sleeping in a comfortable bed with him wasn't going to hurt anyone.

Babs had encouraged her to do what she felt best for the child while she made dinner for the adults. Cassie had lain with him holding her hand as he let sleep finally take over. Adam came in to let her know dinner was ready, staring at his sleeping son. She waited for him to say more but he held out his hand to help her up and walked her down to a quiet meal with the family, everyone mindful of what was ahead.

After dinner that night they sat in the living room. Cassie glanced at Clay, mindful that he was the sheriff, not just Daniel's uncle. She'd agreed that he would ask the questions and she would answer everything she could. For some stupid reason, she'd even agreed to Kate, his wife, recording the conversation just so she didn't have to go repeating herself. Eli had approved it and he sat with a glass of whiskey near the fireplace.

Clay smiled at her, doing his best to make her relax. She got it, she'd used the same approach with many of her clients to win their trust. Women who present at shelters usually came with so much excess baggage, that it was a hard slog to gain their trust but she was there for it. She could hardly complain if he used the same tactics to get what he wanted.

But being on the receiving end had her questioning herself.

"Tell me how you met Daniel's mother."

A day she would never forget. "It was about 9 months ago. She came into the women's shelter begging for help. Said her husband beat her and Daniel and she was terrified he was going to come and drag her back home." She ignored the sudden intake of breath from Adam.

Clay held up his hand toward his brother. It'd been agreed on earlier that he would keep his voice to himself or leave the room. Clay wanted the whole story in one go so he could decide what action he was going to take if any. "Can you please clarify your position at the shelter."

"I'm a trained psychologist. I think that's self-explanatory." She stared at him, and he smiled.

"Thank you. Please continue, Cassie."

She took a breath. "I'm afraid I was hesitant at first to take her in because our spaces are so limited. We have to be particularly choosey with who we house. It's part of my job that I hate but there it is. There was something about her, something I couldn't put my finger on." Even now Cassie still berated herself over it. How she didn't see through the façade that Lissa had built around her. "You have to understand, we have limited funding and too many people needing what little we have so it becomes challenging to accept those that need us most and weed them out from the ones who can manage on their own."

Clay tilted his head, glancing at his wife and then back to Cassie. "What made you change your mind?"

"I saw she had a child in the car, that was it for me. We gave her a room and did what we could to help her. She became one of ours and we do everything we can to get them in a place where they can cope on their own and support themselves."

Grandpa rocked in his chair near the fire, watching quietly. Cassie had already taken a shine to the old man. He was kind and gentle and she felt she could trust him if she needed to.

"Did you know she was a drug addict?"

Cassie shook her head. "No. That's always a deal breaker for us. We don't have the facilities for that kind of care. We try to direct them to another organization."

"Did you know she had taken Daniel without permission?"

Cassie did a slow blink and sighed. "Do you really think I would have taken this long to bring him back if I did?" She was tired of these questions already, but she still had so much to tell them. "Look, how about you just let me talk. We'll get to the meaty bits far quicker, if you don't mind."

A smile twitched at Kate's lips and Cassie almost felt like

they shared a moment together. She sent her a silent 'thank you.'

"Fine. If you'd rather, go ahead."

Cassie glanced around the room, her gaze resting on Adam who sat near his grandfather. This was going to hurt him, but she consoled herself with the fact that she had saved his son.

"I got to know Lissa and Daniel slowly over time. One of the rules of the refuge is they must attend sessions with me. I'm a clinical psychologist, specializing in children and youths and it's my job to offer therapy to support our residents and risk assessment, I report to the team weekly about my findings. Everything is confidential within the house, but we get to share information that will help the women move forward. From housing to jobs, to legal help with a lawyer we have on board for domestic violence, property settlements, it's all there for them. If they choose to use it."

She remembered the first time she'd made an appointment with Lissa. The woman had balked and refused to be 'attacked by a shrink.' Her words. Cassie had eventually talked her into a session but only after laying down the rules which would see her removed from the refuge if she didn't comply. She'd tried every trick in the book. Outright defiance, sulking and when those didn't work, she tried the tears.

Cassie had seen it all before. The emotions that ran through some of the people she helped were more than justified. But Lissa didn't seem to fit any of the profiles Cassie had seen in research or practice. She was hard to pin down even though she insisted she was a battered wife. She had scars she showed to prove her point but some of the common indicators shared by victims of abuse weren't present with Lissa, there was something that didn't feel right to Cassie. Cassie had a great nose for lies and it hadn't let her down yet.

"Once I made it clear that she had to attend, some with Daniel, some just alone, we began to get along better. She has a way about her that is quite endearing, and... I liked her." Cassie swallowed hard, "She was an attentive mother from what I could see. Once we placed her in accommodation outside the refuge, I continued to visit to keep any eye on them both and we had our sessions at her home."

It was there that Cassie began to see the cracks forming. She shook her head, the vision of the last time she saw the house burned into her brain. Sweat beaded on her top lip and her heart started to race and her whole body began to tremble uncontrollably.

Kate crouched in front of her, taking her hands. "Cassie. You're safe, okay? Nothing is going to hurt you here." She stared into her eyes until Cassie nodded, doing her best to slow her breathing.

"I'm right here and I'm not going to let anything happen to you."

Eli hurried over and handed her his whiskey. "Take a sip and take your time."

She gripped the glass in a shaky hand and lifted it to her lips. The fiery liquid burned down her throat making her gasp and cough. She handed it back to him and wiped a hand over her eyes.

Eli stood behind her chair, one hand on her shoulder as she gathered herself.

Adam went to stand, a pained expression on his face, but his father put a hand on his arm. "Sit, son. Looks like things are just getting interesting. Poor girl ain't going to want to repeat herself, I'm thinking."

The voices floated around her, and she stared at them,

one by one, reminding herself that she got Daniel out. He was safe thanks to her. Nothing these people could say would take that away from her. She'd done the right thing.

She cleared her throat. "I began to suspect Daniel was being mistreated but I couldn't pin it down. He seemed happy. There were no visible signs of injury, and he wasn't acting frightened."

She closed her eyes for a second, willing the words to come easier. "Lissa got a job. She said she was making deliveries for a local restaurant and could take Daniel with her. It seemed to be working well, and I was pleased for her."

Cassie took a shuddering breath. "But one day I called in and she wasn't there. Daniel was alone."

***

Adam gripped the chair with both hands and his father patted his shoulder.

"Where was she?" His voice was quiet and cold. He knew more than anyone what she was like. He lived with her for long enough to discover that the only person she cared about was herself. It still confounded him why she took Daniel in the first place.

Cassie stared him in the eye. "I don't know. I was about to take Daniel with me back to the refuge when she came back. Oh, she was sorry. Couldn't stop talking about how she just had to run out for just a second and didn't want to wake him from his afternoon nap."

Adam swallowed the bitterness rising in his throat. His son would have been terrified alone. "She was high, wasn't she?"

"I wasn't one hundred percent sure that time but eventually I figured it out."

"Why didn't you call the police?"

She took a shuddering breath and stared him in the eye.

"I wasn't sure. I suspected she was using but she was good at covering up the clues, you know?"

Adam snorted. He knew better than anyone how his ex-wife could fool the best. He lived with her for long enough and didn't figure it out. He nodded, nausea rising in his throat. His son had been living with a drug addict for so long. How was he going to make that up to Daniel?

"I decided it was in Daniel's best interests if I could get closer to her. Try and become her friend, not just her counsellor. If I'd called the police then, there was no knowing what would have happened to Daniel. I wasn't prepared to let him get lost in the system. I would have had no control over his future if that happened and back then I didn't know what I do now."

Grandpa sniffed. "Thank you from the bottom of our hearts for that."

Cassie shrugged it off, but Adam wasn't convinced she was blameless in all of this. Not yet. "Surely you had some resources that you could use to protect him. He's just a child."

"We live in a challenging area, Mr. Wilson. Our recourses were limited, and I did what I could with what I had which, I have to admit are dismal compared to what is available in this state."

His father spoke. "Nobody has asked where you were, where you found Daniel."

Cassie glanced at them with resignation in her eyes. "South Texas Border, San Antonio."

His heart sank. One of the most notorious drug routes in the country from Mexico. He wiped a hand over his face and swallowed the lump in his throat. Why wasn't he surprised.

"She was involved with them, wasn't she? The drug runners?"

6

The image of what she'd walked into was burned into her brain. She couldn't unsee it. The blood on the kitchen floor, smears of it on the kitchen counter as if someone had tried to grab it as a means to support themselves.

She swallowed the bile burning up her throat and focused on details to gain control. "You need to hear the full story. Not just the bit where I took Daniel."

Babs came down the stairs on quiet feet. Cassie glanced at her, and she smiled. "He's asleep, sugar, his teddy clutched tight in his fist. I sat with him long enough to think he's out for the night. Don't worry. I'll keep an ear out for him."

Cassie tucked a strand of hair behind her ear. Letting him out of her sight was hard after what they'd gone through. Babs came into the lounge and took a seat opposite, giving Cassie a reassuring smile. "Go ahead, sugar. Don't let me stop you."

Having the woman close seemed to soothe her and Lord knows she needed it. Being support for everyone in the last few years had taken its toll on her well-being and she was almost at burn out stage. Her boss had warned her when she first started that this industry could send you to burn out quicker than any other. Dealing with other people's problems wasn't easy. Having a Babs in her life would have been amazing. She wondered if the family knew how lucky they were to have her in their lives. Cassie could only dream of being so lucky.

"Living in that area, you get to know who the drug runners are soon enough, and which cartel owns what part of town and what to do to avoid them. And before you say I should have found somewhere better to live, my parents tell me the same thing every week." She took a moment to breathe and to remind herself that she was doing the right thing even if it wasn't what her parents wanted for her. "But those women needed me. Their children needed me. I felt I could do more in that area after I did a placement there fresh out of college."

She'd be the first to admit how terrified she'd been when she arrived in town. Her parents had tried to talk her out of it, but she insisted poor people needed her as much as anyone. Besides, this was the only post she was offered, and she wasn't about to turn it down. Once her degree was complete, she headed back and had been there ever since.

"I enjoyed my work, but the drug lords are getting stronger, less concerned about who sees them and more focused on finding new ways to traffic into big cities. They don't care who they hurt, so long as they make the money."

Adam dropped his head into his hands.

"I expressed my concern to my supervisor but without some sort of proof we had nothing. Lissa covered her tracks well. But one day I was driving past her house, and I saw a truck I recognized. It belonged to a man named Raoul Estefan."

"Crap." Clay Wilson shook his head. "Are you certain?"

If a small-time sheriff knew who he was, chances are Raoul was a bigger dealer than she'd thought. "Positive. We keep an unofficial list in the office of people we know to avoid just for our own personal safety. Sadly, some of them are now going incognito so they could be anybody. It's quite the challenge some days."

Kate put a hand on Clay's arm. "Back to Raoul. How come you know about him?"

Clay stood and started pacing the room. "Because I think he's trying to get a foothold in our territory, that's why. Between me and the Dallas office, we have been tracking him for ages. Picked up a couple of his boys but could never seem to get him this far up into our net." He stood facing Cassie. "He may not be the head of that cartel but he's the top man as far as we're concerned. You know how dangerous this guy is, right?"

She blanched and nodded, her stomach unsettled, the blood strong in her memory. "I'm starting to."

Clay crouched down in front of her. "You did good getting away from him, Cassie. It could easily have gone very wrong."

She swallowed the bile rising in her throat. "I think it did."

***.

"What do you mean?" Adam couldn't keep quiet any longer. The more she got into the story, the more questions he had.

"Lissa was starting to change, and I worried about her and Daniel. She had more money than a delivery driver made but she just brushed me off if I said anything about it.

Claimed it was tips, but I knew the area well and the people that lived here. The only ones who tip like that are drug lords and people involved with them. Rich people don't live in that town. Not if they have any sense of safety anyway. Easy to get a pizza with special toppings, if you know what I mean."

Cassie leaned back into Eli's touch as if he soothed her and finally Adam understood why his brother was here and he was grateful. They shared a glance and Adam nodded his thanks.

"She was getting more erratic too. Forgetting appointments and trying to brush me off. Daniel was being left alone more and more. I tried to talk to her about it and she snapped one day. Said I had no idea the pressure she was under. That I'd never understand because I was too proper and had money, parents that would bail me out if anything went wrong. She called me soft. That hurt."

Babs tsked. "Oh child, you're just perfect the way you are. That girl could never settle down here no matter what we all did for her."

Cassie gave a quick smile, but the frown returned. "One day she had a split lip and a bruise down one side of her face. Daniel acted skittish around me which was unusual too. She'd been beaten but refused to acknowledge that. Said she tripped over Daniel's toys because he always left them out and no matter how many times she told him, he never cleaned up."

Cassie sighed and swallowed, taking a moment to gather herself.

"Did you ever see any bruises on my son?" Adam gripped his hands together, his short nails digging into his palms as he waited for an answer.

Cassie shook her head, and the tension eased a little.

"Nothing serious, a few here and there but she wasn't beating him. He was dirty some of the time as if he hadn't had a bath for a few days and I know he was hungry because he told me so." That was when she had begun to visit more regularly and always carried items like muesli bars and fruit for Daniel.

"She was earning all this money, and she didn't buy him food?" What was Lissa thinking? Why did she even take their son if she wasn't prepared to look after him? It was for spite, plain and simple. Adam knew that. And the child had bruises now so he knew that along the way, she'd gotten more careless around their son.

"The day I took him was the scariest day of my life."

Adam moved forward in his chair and noticed everyone in the room focus on Cassie with undivided attention.

"I was trying to call in every other day just to keep an eye on Daniel. I wanted to come more, but when I tried Lissa threatened to run or hide him so I wouldn't have access. I couldn't risk that, I didn't have evidence of abuse or enough to claim neglect, so I had nothing to go to the authorities with. I also didn't want to risk Daniel getting swallowed by the system. The drug lords use the foster system in that area to find kids for runners and as cover for their smugglers. I just couldn't risk it." She squeezed her eyes shut for a second, seeming to collect herself, before she continued. "Lissa said I should have been his mother because I made more fuss than she did. Daniel was sitting on the front step crying when I arrived." She took the tissue that Kate offered her but gripped it in her hands, letting the tears flow down her cheeks unheeded.

"There was blood on his face. I grabbed him and checked him over. Even his teddy had blood on it."

Clay spoke up. "Let me guess, it wasn't his?"

"You guessed it. I put him in my car, told him to stay put and be quiet and I went inside. I had to know if Lissa was okay." She closed her eyes and kept them shut while she told them the rest of the story. "The house had been trashed. Every piece of furniture had been up ended, cushions ripped apart and cupboards opened and emptied onto the floor. I walked into the kitchen. Blood was on the tiles, lots of it. When I saw the smears on the wall near the phone, I freaked out. Lissa wasn't there."

"What did you do, Cassie?"

She continued with a tremor in her voice. "I went into her bedroom, terrified she was there but I had to know. I couldn't leave her there if she was still alive. I had to help."

Now the tears were pouring down her cheeks and the sobs were getting louder.

"The blood was everywhere. Handprints smeared down the wall in the hallway, a congealed puddle of blood on the dirty white tiles. Someone had walked through it. Tiny footprints. Daniel had been in here and seen it." Her voice faded as she gulped, the fear she felt then hitting her in the solar plexus again. Adam saw her face pale. "The smell of blood. It was everywhere." She held a hand over her mouth, and he watched the muscles in her throat work as she remembered.

Adam licked his lips before asking the question. "Was she there?"

Cassie shook her head. "No. But someone else was."

7

The thought of opening the door and seeing a body was almost enough to make her leave and go far far away. But a noise came from the bedroom and her conscience wouldn't let her walk away. What if Lissa was in there and hurt? She couldn't just ignore that. She put her hand on the door handle, sticky with blood.

As long as she lived, Cassie would never forget the fear that galvanized her out of that house when the young man glanced up from ransacking the mattress and saw her.

"I ran. I was terrified and knew if he caught me I was done for." She hiccupped as a sob rose. "I was fast, but I was careful. I wasn't going to face the same fate as Lissa. I avoided the blood puddle in the hallway and jumped over it." How she'd even registered that at the time amazed her now she had time to think about it. "He wasn't so lucky. I heard his footsteps as he pounded after me and then he slipped and crashed. It gave me the precious extra seconds I needed to get out of there." She wiped a hand up her throat, desperate to finish the story and put it out of her mind.

"I never went home. I just got in my car and drove.

Daniel was terrified and kept calling out for his daddy. I drove through the night and once we were across the border, I drove until we found a cheap hotel off the beaten track. Figured if we could hide and work out the next move, we had a good chance of staying alive."

Clay cleared his throat before he spoke. "You did good, Cassie."

Adam stood and walked closer. "How did you figure out he was my son?"

It wasn't that hard to put together once they both felt safe away from the chaos. "It was a combination of things. When I sensed Lissa was lying to me, I'd pulled up the details she provided when we took her in. Some of it didn't feel right and it led me to investigate her past and came up with quite a checkered history. I searched Daniel's birth records and found your name and one thing led to another. The story of his abduction was everywhere at the time. Plus, Daniel kept talking about the ranch and how much he missed the animals. I figured if he was that keen to come back, either Lissa was lying, or you both kept the abuse from him. Once we were safe, I searched you more and found the name of the ranch and put it all together."

Adam's lip quivered and he held back the tears. "So you know she stole him from me?"

"Yeah. I knew there was more to her story as I already said but I wasn't expecting this."

His tears rolled over his lashes and ran down his stubbled cheeks. Adam glanced up at the stairs and smiled. "Thank you." It was the most heartbreaking smile she had ever seen. So raw and full of desperation. It made her heart ache, she averted her eyes not wanting to see all that emotion directed at her in that way. It was too much.

Clay got her attention. "Did you recognize the young man in the bedroom?"

She did, he was on their list of people to avoid. "Yeah. The guy you were talking about. Raoul. He saw my face too but I'm quick when I need to be. Track and field in college. It was automatic to go as fast as I did. I slammed the door and ran for my life. All I could think about was getting me and Daniel as far away as I could." She stared at her hands held in her lap, "Finding Adam felt like my only option... And here we are." She began to shake then, the enormity of what they'd escaped and what she'd done finally hitting home.

Arms wrapped around her, and she smelled the sweet perfume of Babs. "I've got you, sugar. It's going to be okay. There, there." She held her as Cassie cried her heart out. Partly from fear, partly from relief that she was safe now. The few days on the road had been the worst days of her life. Permanently terrified and constantly looking over her shoulder as she made her way to Wishbone, always worried that they would be stopped and returned or worse.

When her sobs subsided, she sat up, mopping her eyes with the mangled tissue. "I'm sorry. I'm not usually an emotional or weak person. I didn't mean to lose it then."

Babs brushed the hair back from her face and stared into her eyes. "Sugar, you're one of the strongest people I have had the pleasure to meet, and I sincerely mean that. Not everyone would take on a drug cartel to save a child they hardly knew. You have our gratitude and anything you need, is yours. You hear me now? Anything."

"It takes guts to do what you did, Cassie." Kate ran her hand down Cassie's arm. "Most people freeze in situations like this and get themselves killed."

Clay patted her on the shoulder. "Looks like our Cassie

isn't your average human. I can't thank you enough for what you did. I'm going to get you to come down to the station with Eli in the next couple of days, okay? I want to go through this again without the emotion we've all shown tonight and get a timeline done. Are you okay with that?"

Our Cassie. They had taken her on face value and accepted her. All it had taken was escaping a drug cartel and a rescued child. Did she really want to be accepted as one of them after all she'd gone through?

"Stop overthinking, Cassie." Kate pushed a fresh tissue into her hand. "This family is very welcoming. You're one of us now, so accept it. It's just their way, okay?"

Cassie pushed herself to her feet, feeling crowded in with everyone hovering over her. She'd never suffered claustrophobia before but ever since she'd taken Daniel, being anywhere confined activated her fight or flight instinct and made her anxious. She took a few steps backward, trying to find the space she desperately needed.

"Cassie." Adam stood beside her, his face ragged and tear stained. She turned to him and found herself enveloped in his arms, his body shaking with sobs. Her need for space evaporated, replaced with a longing to comfort him and be comforted in return. She slid her arms around his waist and hugged him, muttering soothing sounds as he wept. "Shh, it's okay, Adam. He's safe now."

They clung to each other, two people joined by the love of a child. The warm, earthy smell of him lingered on clothes and she found her body relaxing into his embrace more fully. Being this close to Adam was making her anxious but in a different way than the rest of the family had. She closed her eyes and rested her cheek against his shirt, the smell of hay and animals as soothing as the hard chest she rested against. It took her all of five seconds to worry about how this would look to anyone watching them. She tensed.

***.

As soon as Adam noticed Cassie tense, he cleared his throat and let her go. She stepped back, her cheeks glowing a pretty shade of pink. He hadn't held a woman in his arms for years and it was a revelation to him. When she'd arrived, he'd been ready to crucify her for having his son, but now he knew the story, he wanted to give her everything he had to show her how grateful he was. He couldn't get over how brave she was, especially when Daniel wasn't her blood. That was one gutsy woman right there.

"Sorry, I didn't mean to overwhelm you. We're all kinda emotional, right now."

She gave him a shy smile. "It was good to get that off my chest. Thank you all for giving me the time to ease into the conversation. I know it must have been hard for you to be patient when you wanted answers."

A child's scream pierced the air and both Adam and Cassie bolted up the stairs together. The door to Adam's old bedroom was open and the bathroom light on. Daniel sat with his back against the headboard, screaming.

Cassie reached him first. She climbed up on the bed and gathered his son in her arms, rocking him. "It's okay, baby, I'm here. I'm here." She held him tight as he buried his face into her chest. His little fists clinging to her shirt like he was scared to let her go. "You're safe, baby," over and over she repeated the mantra, as she hugged him, stroking a loving hand over his hair and down his arms. Daniel's screams slowly subsided to an occasional sob. All the while, Adam stood by watching as she worked her magic on his son.

When it seemed as though Daniel was calmer, Adam moved closer to the bed, leaning in to put a hand on his son's back, desperate to grab hold of him and give him the hug he'd been dreaming about but still wary he would frighten him more. "You're safe here, son. Everything is going to be okay. You're safe now, I promise you."

Daniel lifted his face from Cassie's chest and peeked at him with tear filled eyes.

"Dad...Daddy?"

His heart melted at the words. Daniel held out his hand and Adam wrapped his fingers around his sons. He sank down on the bed next to Cassie and kept his son's hand in his. This is what he'd longed for the last three years. To see his son, be part of his life and watch him fall asleep. "You're safe here, Daniel. Cassie and I will take care of you."

He blinked as tears ran down his cheeks. "P...pr...romise?"

Cassie glanced at Adam, her eyes filled with worry.

"I promise. You're home now and you're not going anywhere again, not without me." He cleared his throat. "Cassie and I will take care of you."

8

Had he just tied her into taking care of his son? Cassie chewed on her lip as she watched Daniel fall asleep, his hand holding hers in a death grip. When his fingers became slack, she eased off the bed.

Adam spoke from the shadow of the big armchair near the window. "I think you should stay here now. If he wakes up again, I don't want him upset any more than he is already. It's going to take enough for him to get over this as it is."

She nodded. Her body was so tired it ached, and she was mentally and emotionally exhausted, her brain was so muddled she could sleep anywhere. She and Daniel had shared a bed every night since they had run because both were scared and didn't want to be alone. Now they were safe, Cassie wanted to sleep away her life.

"I need a shower and a hot drink. Then sleep. I could sleep for a week." She didn't have anything to change into. The only clothes she had were the ones she was wearing and a spare set she had brought for her and Daniel on the road. Both were dirty. She held her arms out self-consciously looking at the crumpled, sweat stained shirt and jeans she'd worn on and off for the last week. Washing them in the hotel room's sink hadn't done the job she'd hoped for and stopping too often to buy fresh clothes made her too scared. One change each she'd picked up at a small tourist stop when she was zig zagging her way to the ranch had to suffice, and she'd dealt with it as best she could. Shopping at Walmart or similar had been too stressful for her with Daniel in tow. The thought of him saying something and her not being able to defend them both had kept her awake at night.

"I don't have anything clean to put on. Neither of us do."

Adam touched her on the arm. "Leave it with me." He hurried out of the room, and she heard his footsteps on the stairs.

Moments later Babs bustled past the door and went into another room down the hallway. Cassie heard her opening and closing drawers.

Babs popped her head in the room with a bundle of clothing. "Here you are, Sugar. Our Ella is about your size so these should fit just fine. The undergarments still have tags on them so feel free to use what you want." She walked into the bathroom and put them on the counter. She opened a drawer and showed Cassie. "Plenty of fresh toiletries here. Help yourself."

"I'm going to sleep here with Daniel. I think it's for the best since we've spent the last few nights together and he trusts me. I don't want him scared during the night if he wakes again."

"Agreed, sugar. He trusts you and so do we. Can I get you something while you shower? Adam said you wanted a drink."

"I'd just about kill for an herbal tea." She groaned when

she realized what she'd said but Babs only patted her on the arm and walked to the door.

"Consider it done. Now go clean up and let that hot water ease some of that tension out of your body. The shower in there is pretty amazing." She walked away and Cassie headed to the bathroom, pushing the door to but not quite closed.

She turned on the shower, stripped off her dirty clothes and stepped under the rain shower head, sighing in pleasure at the thought of not having to put on the same clothes again. They stunk of fear and sweat. Cassie stood under the soothing spray, savoring the luxury of not having to worry that she needed to be quick and on guard. Someone else could deal with knocks on the door and questions. Not that she had dealt with any on their trip, but the idea it could happen had made her very conscious of her time management and responsibilities.

Lathering her hair with the shampoo in the shower felt more luxurious than she could imagine. The hint of lavender and citrus helped clear the fog in her brain and by the time she had washed away all traces of dirt she felt like a new person.

Cassie flicked off the shower and stepped out, grabbing the big fluffy towel and wrapped it around herself. She toweled her hair dry and glanced in the mirror. Her eyes were ringed in dark shadows and no matter how much she tried to relax her jaw, the tension still showed. She could feel the taught muscles up her cheeks into her skull, throbbing and making her feel lightheaded.

A noise from the bedroom startled her.

"Just me, sugar. I have your herbal tea and a snack. I'll just leave them here. Shout out if you need anything else.

Jack and I are in the room at the end of the hallway. See you in the morning."

"Thank you, Babs. Appreciate it."

"Not as much as we appreciate you, girl. Don't forget that. Night now."

***.

"How is she, Mama?" Adam stood near the stairs, anxious to see his son again but worried that he would be overstepping the line for now.

"She's having a shower, son. It's going to be fine. I promise." Mama patted him on the arm as she walked past and went to sit near Grandpa.

"Why don't you sleep here tonight, Adam?" His father sat with his hands over his belly, contemplating his eldest son. "Go grab your gear and sleep in Clay's room. That way you can be here if Daniel needs you."

He wanted that more than anything, to be close to his son. "I'm not sure I'd know what to do. It's been so long, and he's focused on Cassie. After what she did to bring him home, I don't want to get in her way."

Mama smiled at him and he felt like a five-year-old again who didn't understand basic instructions.

"Yes, Mama. I get it. One step at a time. I'll be right back." He strode into the kitchen and out the door toward the shared men's accommodation. He usually loved hanging out with the farm hands in the bunk house but tonight he wanted to be close to his son.

He stopped and gazed at the stars, his chest exploding with so many emotions he didn't know if he was going to be able to hold it in. For years he'd been waiting for this moment, but it was nothing like the reunion he had in his head. He couldn't believe Cassie putting her life on the line to return Daniel. It just went to show there were still good people out there.

How was he ever going to repay her for what she'd done? Anything she wanted she could have. It went without question.

As he walked down to the bunk house, he wondered if she'd given any thought to returning to her job. Chances are it wouldn't be possible because she would have a target on her back. The family would support her until she got back on her feet if that's what she wanted to do. It was going to take some time to work through this and he just hoped that she would be willing to stay on the ranch and let Daniel acclimate to being back before she decided it was time to get on with her own life.

Maybe he could offer her a job as a companion, it would keep her safe and his son happy.

He grabbed his bathroom gear, a pair of sleep boxers and a change of clothes for tomorrow and headed back to the main house.

9

Cassie sat in Clay's office, her hands gripped tightly on her lap. She'd refused to bring Daniel with her. In her professional opinion, it was too soon. And to be sitting in front of the sheriff like this would be too traumatic for him, even if it was someone he vaguely knew. Better they try to bring it into a normal conversation if he didn't willingly offer it up himself.

Leaving him at the ranch had been hard. He'd whined when she said she had to go and leave him, tears had threatened, and she'd almost decided to stay when Babs had come to the rescue and tempted Daniel with helping her bake his favorite cookies. Adam had added to the joy of staying behind by talking about the baby chickens that needed feeding. She'd watched the glimmer in Daniel's eyes as he pondered the possibilities. Cassie had encouraged him by giving him the option to make up his own mind.

"Perhaps I should stay and feed the chickens, Adam. I'm not sure Daniel is the right person for the job. He doesn't have much experience."

He'd jumped off the stool and ran to his father, stopping beside him. "I do. I know I can do it. Please, Cassie?"

She took a few seconds to think over her decision and then nodded. "If you're sure, Daniel."

He clapped his hands and Adam winked at her over his son's head.

Now she was here, she wished she could have stayed at the ranch. Telling this story over and over was doing nothing to soothe her nerves. If anything, it was making it clear to her just how much danger she had avoided.

"They were obviously looking for something. Any idea what that might have been?"

She shook her head. "I have no idea. I wasn't Lissa's confident now that I look back on the relationship. She used me to get what she wanted, nothing more."

"And the guy in the bedroom didn't utter a word?"

She shivered remembering the way he'd looked at her. Cold, calculating and plain evil. If she'd stayed, she would be dead by now. She had no doubt about it. "If he did, I didn't hear him over the pounding of my heart. I was terrified and my only thought was to get out and save Daniel." She wiped her hands over her face, trying to hold back the tears but it was no good. So much emotion had been held in while they ran and now it was coming out.

Clay pushed a box of tissues toward her. "I know it's hard, Cassie. But I need to know anything you can remember."

He held up a sheet of paper with a man's face on it and she couldn't stop the gasp of fear that escaped her mouth. The dark glint of menace in his eyes, the sneer on his lips and the scar running from his eyebrow to his lip made her stomach churn. "Definitely the man you saw?"

With her hand over her mouth, she nodded. "That's

him." She'd never forget him as long as she lived. He was in her dreams, nightmares really. She blushed remembering last night how she'd scared the heck out of Adam when she'd screamed in her sleep, and he'd come racing in.

Clay leaned back in his chair and stared at her.

"What?" Cassie felt her skin prickle as he watched her. Adam's father, Jack Jnr put a hand on her shoulder and squeezed, trying to comfort her. When Cassie had proposed Daniel stay with his grandmother, Grandpa had jumped in and offered to support her at the interview, and she was grateful. One small step to getting Daniel to rely on the rest of the family and not just her.

"Raoul Estefan. I don't want to scare you, but you need to know what these guys are capable of. Last night I said we've had some dealings with them. They're trying to get a foot hold in the Texas hill country and it's up to me and the other Sherriff's offices in the local areas to stop them. We've already had a couple of run ins with them. They're dangerous, Cassie. They aren't afraid to flaunt their violence and from what we've seen from them, they're persistent. The normal deterrence have slowed their growth down but it hasn't stopped them."

"You think he's going to come looking for me, don't you?" Bright lights twinkled around her eyes and her heart started to race. *It isn't over, they're going to come after us.*

"Breath, girl, you're safe with us." Mr. Wilson crouched so he was looking into her eyes and gripped her hands in his. "We got plenty of men on the ranch to keep an eye on things so don't go getting yourself all fussed up, you hear?"

She wanted to believe him.

"My boys are used to patrolling the boundary fences and chasing off cattle rustlers and they're always armed. We've had more than our share of trouble with illegals too and know how to deal with it. Nobody, but nobody is going to get onto our property, I can assure you of that. Now stop fretting and leave the security to me and Clay here."

"Dad is right. You'll be safe at the ranch."

His calm voice didn't do anything to stop the wild beating of her heart. "But what if he's after me or Daniel? What am I going to do?"

"We will protect you and Daniel, don't go worrying about that. I want to know what they're after. Did Lissa have drugs that she wasn't turning over or was there money she had stashed, and he was looking for? They'll kill for less."

"You're not making things any easier, son." Mr. Wilson admonished his son.

"Dad, we need to keep this real. Cassie has to know the danger she's in. It's only fair to be prewarned, don't you think?"

"I guess you're right, but I don't like it. Last thing we need is that kind of people around our town." He squeezed Cassie's arm and took his seat again.

"I firmly believe forewarned is forearmed. These guys don't play nice. She was there, in the house. So as far as they're concerned, she is involved with whatever Lissa is doing. Being it selling drugs or encroaching on their territory, who cares. If they didn't find whatever it was they were looking for at Lissa's, they might think Cassie has it or will be able to help them find it. If she was holding out on them, be it money or drugs, they'll do whatever it takes to get it back."

"Tell me what to do." She lifted her head and stared at him. This wasn't going to go away just because she didn't want to think about it. They'd survived this far, they could manage whatever came at them. The irony of her favorite podcast came unbidden and she smiled.

"What?" Clay stared at her.

"Would you believe I listen to true crime podcasts to zone out when I'm in my car or going to sleep and now I find myself in the middle of something worthy of a serial of its own." She muffled the hysterical giggle that threatened with a cough.

He stared at his father before looking back at her.

"Stay at the ranch if possible, don't come to town alone. Always be aware of your surroundings. I know you don't know anyone in town, but you know what this guy looks like. I expect him to be looking for you as he's already made you."

When she stared at him blankly, he clarified his comment.

"He knows what you look like, where you worked, probably everything about you. If you get any spidery senses or see something out of the ordinary, tell someone. I don't care if you feel silly reporting it, just do it. Your gut instinct has kept you and Daniel alive so far. Trust it."

"Okay. Anything else?"

Clay leaned forward. "Your cell phone. Is it yours or a work one supplied to you?"

She frowned. "Mine. Why?"

"It's way too easy to track anyone these days. Do you mind if I have a look at the settings?"

She handed it over. "Sure."

While he checked out her cell he continued. "Just to be on the safe side, send an email from an untraceable address to your work saying you're taking emergency extended leave for family reasons. It won't stop them from looking for you, but it will keep authorities out of things in case a coworker decides to report you missing. I wouldn't be at all surprised if the police in that town aren't corrupt. Cartels are adept at paying off those around them."

***.

Adam was standing in the kitchen having coffee when his father arrived back with Cassie. Daniel jumped from his chair and ran to her, wrapping his arms around her waist.

She shared a glance with him, and he felt the jolt in his stomach. She looked as though she'd had the worst morning imaginable, and the tiredness was back, heavy dark circles marred under her eyes. After last night when he'd gone in to check on her, he finally understood just how much this was affecting her.

Cassie's higpitched scream had ripped him from sleep and sent him bolting for his old room. She'd been thrashing in the blankets, and he sat down on the edge of the bed, wondering how long it would be before she woke Daniel. He reached out and touched her arm, making her startle even more. He stroked her arm, speaking in soothing tones until she slowed her thrashing. Eventually she settled down and it was then that she opened her eyes. "Adam?"

"It's okay, Cassie. You were dreaming. You're safe."

She glanced over at Daniel who slept with his hands tucked under his chin, his ragged teddy close by.

"You're both okay. Go back to sleep." He'd glanced around the room to make sure there was nobody else there, more for her sake than his. He knew the house was locked up tight and security set.

She'd given him a quick smile and closed her eyes. Within minutes she was sleeping.

He put his coffee down and walked over to her, putting a hand on her back. "Come have a coffee. Looks like you could use it. Clay a bit rough, was he?"

She let out a shuddering sigh and moved to the kitchen

island and took a seat. She rested her head in her hands for a moment, taking a few deep breaths before looking at him. "Clay was only doing his job, but it was a bit intense, yes."

Babs poured her a coffee and pushed it over toward her. "Here you go, sugar, get that down you and I'll fix some lunch."

"I'm not sure I could eat anything." Pinched lines around her mouth showed white as she cradled her coffee. Adam wished he could do more to help her because at the end of the day, she was in this predicament because of his family.

"Food fixes everything in this house." Adam picked up his coffee and took a sip. "Least that's what Mama thinks."

"Nothing that can't be sorted out over a meal. Chicken quesadilla's okay for y'all?"

Daniel clapped his hands and grinned. His boy was feeling better this morning and having the time with him while Cassie was in town was the happiest Adam had been in years. He knew it was important to give Daniel space to acclimate and he didn't want to overwhelm his son so now that Cassie was back, he was heading down to the barn to catch up on work.

"I'll be back later, Mama. Save me a couple, okay?"

She turned around and wiped her hands on her apron. "Can't you wait, Adam? It won't be long."

He wanted to stay but something told him not to push it with Daniel. The child was gravitating to Cassie now she was back which he couldn't blame him for. Even pale and exhausted, she had a warmth about her. He could see why Daniel felt so safe with her. Take it slow, don't swamp him and things will be okay. "I just have to check on the men, Mama. I won't be too long." He reached for his hat from the rack near the door when Daniel spoke.

"Can I come too?"

Adam looked at his son, then Cassie, his breath caught in his chest.

"Please, Daddy."

Cassie nodded and gave him a quick smile.

"Sure. We won't be long Mama." He held his hand out hesitantly, Daniel skipped over to him and gripped it tight. Adam had to swallow the lump that had formed in his throat. He looked up at Cassie, a warm smile on her face. They walked out the door and Daniel paused, glanced back at Cassie, his eyes wide. It was too much for his son to leave the only person he'd felt safe with after being without her most of the morning.

Even though Cassie looked exhausted, she seemed to understand what Daniel needed. She stood and followed them outside. Daniel changed in an instant. He let go of Adams hand and skipped down to the barn where Adams father was talking to Grandpa.

They both looked up and smiled.

"Young Daniel. Nice to see you down here. Just in time to help me collect the eggs." Grandpa picked up a tin pail and handed it to him.

Daniel gave Cassie and Adam a quick glance and reached for it. "I can carry that."

Adam stood beside Cassie and watched as his son and Grandpa went searching for eggs. Cassie moved away and followed behind Daniel, ever protective and watchful. He wondered how long it would be before she told him what Clay said. It was enough to rattle her, and he deserved to know. Perhaps it would be better to get the information from his father since he was there.

His father leaned on the rail and watched Adam watching his son. "Feels good to have him back, don't it, son?"

"Yeah. It really does. Didn't think it was ever going to happen."

"That's some brave young lady you have there. What she did," he shook his head. "Well, it makes me scared for her. Clay is worried too. Said that because they know who she is, they'll be after her now, especially if they didn't find what they were looking for. If they're out of product or cash because of Lissa, Cassie and Daniel are definitely targets. God, I wish I knew what she did to bring this on us. I can't believe she dragged that poor child into that life."

Adam swallowed the lump in his throat. "Have you spoken to the men? They need to be aware of strangers and know what to do. Maybe stop hiring unless we know the person too. I know we need more cowboys for the muster but now's not the time."

"I'll be talking to them tonight when they all come in. If we pull together, we can manage with the men we have. Between us I believe we can keep her and Daniel safe." A frown creased his brow. "I'd be more comfortable if you slept in the house for a bit, make your mama happy too to have you around."

He nodded. The same thought had crossed his mind after last night. He wanted to be near Cassie and Daniel as well in case they needed him.

"Did Clay have any idea what could have happened to Lissa?"

Jack shrugged. "You don't mess with these cartel people, Adam. If she ripped them off or held out on them, her life is worthless. Sad as it is, there's nothing we can do about that." He cleared his throat and watched as Daniel excitedly chased a chicken from the pile of straw in the corner of a stall and discovered a pile of eggs. "They were clearly looking for something and I suspect that she is either hiding drugs or money from them. If that's the case, I reckon we can expect a visit any time soon. It won't take long for them to figure out where Cassie and Daniel are. They're not stupid people. They have contacts everywhere Clay said. If Cassie used a credit card for gas to get here or for a motel, that's enough for them to track her down."

He shook his head, his lip curling in disgust. "They're not having either of them, understand? Nobody is taking my son or Cassie from us. We will do everything in our power to protect the both of them."

Adam stood staring straight ahead. She was one of theirs now. With what she'd done, there was no way she could return to her home base. She wouldn't survive a day back there.

"Does she understand that she can't go back?"

Jack turned to him. "Clay didn't exactly spell it out in so many words, but I understood what he meant. I think young Cassie was too shell shocked to take it all in. When she does, you need to be there for her Adam, you hear me?"

"Yes, sir. Loud and clear." She'd risked her life to save his son. He was going to return the favor.

10

"I need to call my boss and tell her I'm okay." Cassie was sitting in front of the fire, staring at the flames after a lovely relaxing dinner.

Grandpa stared at her. "Can you do that without saying where you are or anything about Daniel?"

She chewed on her bottom lip. He wasn't getting at her, that much she understood. He was just trying to keep them both safe.

"She already knows I had a family emergency. I told her that when I got far enough out of town to take a five-minute breather and gas up. But she will be wondering how I am. We were quite close." She paused a moment, trying to figure out a way to keep everyone happy and them safe. "How about if I don't say where I am, just that I'm safe and don't even mention Daniel." Unless the cartel had been to the office to try and intimidate Lorrie, her boss would have no idea where she was or what she was involved in. She should have called in sick the day after they ran.

Adam leaned forward and looked at her. "Do you think your boss will be safe with this going on? I hate the idea other people are going to be in danger because my ex-wife was involved in something she had no need to be."

"Only one way to find out."

Adam got up and handed her the house phone. "Use this and dial 6 then 7 before her number. It'll keep them from seeing who is calling."

Cassie took the phone and pressed the numbers for Lorrie's home.

"Hello."

"Lorrie, its Cassie."

Lorrie squealed loud enough for everyone to hear her. "Girl, where you been? I've been trying to reach you and you're not home and your cell was going straight to voice-mail. Is everyone okay?"

Cassie leaned back in her chair, tears filling her eyes. Lorrie was the closest thing she had to a best friend, and she hated that she was worried about her. "I'm fine now. Please don't worry."

"Worry? What the heck have you got yourself involved in? I've had the cartel here trying to rattle me, the police wanting to know what I know about Lissa's house. You know they set fire to it, right?" She squeezed her eyes closed. Was Clay right about the police? Were they working hand in hand with the cartel?

"No, I didn't know that."

"Burned to the ground. Please tell me you have the child, Cassie. Please."

She stared at Adam. "He's safe, Lorrie."

A sigh came over the line. "Thank the Lord for that. No sign of his mama but if she's involved with them, I expect she will disappear and never resurface. They torched the house as a warning but they're after you, girl. They've been here a couple of times. I can only ignore them for so long, you know?"

"Don't tell them you've heard from me, Lorrie. You know nothing, ok?"

"Phillip has been at the office too. Said he is concerned for you and to make contact if you can so he can put plans in place to protect you."

The lawyer was kind to worry about her, but Cassie had no plans on going back. An itch niggled down her spine. "How did he know I wasn't there?"

"I have no idea. Someone probably said they hadn't seen you around lately."

"Don't tell him you've heard from me please. Tell nobody. Our lives depend on it."

"This isn't about your family, is it, Cassie? This is about Lissa."

"Please don't ask me questions, Lorrie. Just be happy that I'm okay for now." She squeezed her eyes shut, trying to keep herself together.

"Just stay safe, Cassie. And try to stay in touch. I don't dare go to your house. I expect they're watching it anyway."

"Probably. Honestly, there's nothing there worth your life so stay away. Anything there can be replaced if need be."

"You take care and call me again if you can. Remember I love you, Cassie."

"Love you too, Lorrie." She hung up and stared at the phone. "They've been to the shelter and are putting pressure on her. They burned down Lissa's house as a warning, and I'm sure they've already ransacked my place."

Adam stood and took the phone from her and put it back. "Anything you need, I will personally replace. It's the least I can do after what you've done for me."

Her cheeks heated. "That's not necessary. It was my choice to do what I did."

"Still, I feel responsible."

She had a sudden thought. "My parents."

"What about them?"

She stood and started pacing the loungeroom. "If they go to my house, which they probably already have, they'll go through my things and find out where my parents live."

Grandpa tapped his fingers on the leather arm of the big chair he occupied by the fireplace. "You're worried they'll turn up there and harm them? Call and warn them, Cassie. Tell them the truth and pray they stay safe."

Adam handed her the phone again, her hands shook as she tried to dial. Adam's hand came up to cover hers, "Hey, take a breath, it will be okay." He held her gaze encouragingly as she sucked in a calming breath. She exhaled slowly and placed the call.

"Mom, it's Cassie and I'm safe but somethings happened, and I need you to listen carefully to me."

Adam stayed by her side throughout the whole phone call. By the time she hung up, her eyes were filled with tears. Adam leaned closer and tucked a stray curl behind her ear before catching a tear that trickled down her cheek with his thumb. "This is my fault and I'm sorry, Cassie. What you're going through is my fault."

Cassie stared at him. From an angry father to a caring adult. Adam Wilson was a very kind man. He was nothing like Lissa had made out when they'd had their sessions. She much preferred the man in front of her than the image that had been cast of him.

***.

Adam kissed his sleeping son. "You have no idea how

good it is to have him home, Cassie. I can never repay you for what you did."

She stood beside him gazing down at Daniel who slept like an angel with his teddy clutched in his arms. "I'm glad it worked out well, Adam. I didn't think, I just did what I had to do."

"And now you and your family are in harm's way because of it. I'm glad your folks are away travelling for a while. That's one less thing to worry about."

"It was a relief to find out they weren't at home or easy to track down, to be honest." She grinned. "I had no idea they'd bought a camper. Mom has been talking about it for years, but Dad never seemed to be as enthusiastic as she was. I guess she finally wore him down." She shrugged. "Dad said the apartment was locked up tight and they have a doorman, so nobody is getting in there anyway. We can stop worrying about that for now."

"Next time you speak to them, invite them to visit Wishbone. They can stay here. We have plenty of room and Mama would be in heaven to have more people to fuss over."

Cassie laughed for the first time since he'd met her. "She's amazing. You're so lucky to have her."

He put a hand around her shoulders and turned her to face him. A hint of pink touched her cheeks, and she blinked. "So are you. So brave and fearless."

She dipped her head and rested it on his chest, making his heart race. The embrace seemed natural, almost familiar, but also new and exciting. She was the first woman he'd held in his arms since his ex-wife had left. The first woman who'd stirred his feelings and he was doing his best to decide whether it was because he was grateful to her or if it was more.

"I'd better let you get to bed. It's been a rough couple of days for you. Let's hope you sleep better tonight." He dropped a gentle kiss on her hair and stepped back. "Goodnight Cassie."

She glanced up at him and smiled. "Goodnight Adam. Thank you for everything."

He strode out of the room, giving her one final glance as he closed the bedroom door. He stepped into the bedroom next door and leaned on the closed door. She was touching him in places that had been dormant for years, frozen over with anguish and loss.

He pushed himself to move across the room and stripped off his clothes. As he lay on the bed, he could hear her pottering in the bathroom next door. The shower turned on and the screen closed. He tried not to imagine her in the shower, the water washing over her skin. Adam shook his head. This was not the time to go there.

He'd had her agree to stay for now until Daniel settled in, and she was no longer in danger but already the thought of getting her to stay longer was settling in his mind. Was it merely gratitude that drew him to her? There is no question Cassie was beautiful, but this was starting to feel like more than just physical attraction or desire. Was it because she was a strong independent woman who adored his son already and was prepared to put her life on the line to keep him safe.

The last thing he wanted to do was get into a relationship and find out it was merely gratitude that he'd confused with feelings.

He thumped the pillow and rolled over onto his side as the shower turned off, closing his eyes as he imagined her drying herself with the big soft towels his mother preferred before getting into nightwear and sleeping in his old bed.

11

The next day both Daniel and Cassie mostly slept, catching up on what they'd missed out on. Cassie knew that the stress of the last few days was enough to drain the body and Babs popped in and out bringing them whatever they needed, insisting they have the day to be quiet and rest. They ate breakfast in bed and then she snuggled with Daniel, stroking his hair until he fell asleep again. She woke up a couple of times during the day. Once when Adam glanced in and then again when Babs brought up a dinner tray for them.

"Now don't you go fussing, sugar. I told everyone that you need to catch up on your sleep and I don't want to see you downstairs until tomorrow. You and Daniel have been through a lot and the body needs to heal. Sleep is the best thing for you." She popped the tray on Cassie's lap and waited until she started eating.

"Young Daniel will be hungry when he wakes up. Just shout out and I'll bring him something and if I don't hear from you before I go to bed, I'll leave a tray of snacks on his side of the bed."

"You're too good to me Babs. I really appreciate this." She took a bite of the steak and groaned. It was so good. Juicy and tender.

Babs laughed. "We do our own meat here and we're proud of it." She patted Cassie's arm. "Eat and sleep, sugar. I'll see you tomorrow for breakfast."

Babs called out a cheery good morning as Cassie skipped down the stairs with Daniel's hand in hers. He'd woken up chattering about the ranch and the animals and it was the happiest she'd seen him since she'd known him. The day off sleeping had done them both the world of good. She almost felt like she could face anything now.

"Hello you two. Looks like someone is ready for breakfast. What will it be Cassie, Daniel?" She wiped her hands on her apron and came around to hug her grandson before dropping a kiss on Cassie's cheek.

"Pancakes!" Daniel clapped his hands.

"Manners young man." Babs smiled at him.

"Please Grandma." He gave her a cheeky grin and she grabbed him, pulling him up into her arms.

"You my dear young Daniel, are the best thing I've seen this morning." She buried her face in his neck and smothered him in kisses until he giggled hysterically.

Cassie grinned so hard she thought her face would break. This is where Daniel should have been all along. Now he was back, she hoped the nightmares would recede and he would stop being so scared of everything. It would take time. She knew that better than anyone, but his family was just what he needed.

Babs put him down and gave Cassie a wink. "Coffee, dear girl?"

"Please."

"I see dark circles under those pretty eyes, Cassie. Bad night?"

Heat raced up her cheeks and she looked down at the countertop. "Um, yes. Nightmares, so I was a bit restless."

"You should have called out, sugar."

Cassie licked her lips before answering. "Adam, he, ah, he came in when he heard me scream. He stayed with me until I fell asleep."

Babs nodded but didn't say anything.

Daniel climbed up on the stool beside her, a cheeky grin on his face. "You didn't say thank you."

Cassie laughed. "Yes sir. Thank you, Babs."

Babs placed a coffee in front of Cassie and then poured a glass of milk for Daniel. "Pancakes for you too, Cassie?"

"Thank you, that would be lovely." She sipped her coffee. "Is there anything I can do for you today, Babs? I feel like I need a job to do instead of lazing around."

"Hmm, let me think. Apart from keeping an eye on our main man here, nothing off the top of my head. We should look at school shortly. Daniel is missing out on playing with children his own age."

"I need to discuss that with Adam, but I feel it's best to wait until we settle in more. Maybe find a bit of routine here first."

Babs nodded. "Agreed. Maybe ask Adam if there is something the two of you can do down at the barn. Probably some orphans down there need taking care of, usually is."

Cassie sighed. She was hoping for something she could focus on, something to lose the feeling of being in limbo wasn't sitting well with her. She was used to a hectic schedule, trying to fit everything in. This hanging around doing practically nothing was making her twitchy and out of place.

"Sugar, I get it. You're out of your territory and at a loose end but until we know y'all are safe, you need to stick close to home."

Over breakfast, Cassie broached an idea that was rolling around in her head when she woke up this morning. She'd lain quietly watching Daniel dreaming. Mostly he was fine but every now and then he would start as if he was scared and that was totally to be expected after what he'd gone through over the last few years. What happened when she found him was merely the icing on the cake.

"Babs, do you happen to have any art supplies around the house? Like crayons or pencils or even paints?"

Babs wiped her hands on her apron and leaned on the counter. "I can get some for sure. Young Toby has a heap in the cottage. Duke and Cora are away on holiday with him right now and I know they wouldn't mind if you helped yourself to them. How about I take you down there after you finish your breakfast, and you can take what you need?"

Cassie dabbed her lips with the napkin, giving Daniel a quick glance before she answered. "Sounds perfect. I'm thinking some art therapy would be a great idea and it might help someone with their sleep."

Babs glanced at her grandson and nodded. "His daddy mentioned something about that and that you weren't sleeping so great either." She reached out, giving Cassie's hand a gentle squeeze. "Since you're the expert, we'd really appreciate any help you can give him. The last few years must have been pretty traumatic for him. They were for us. I can assure you of that sugar."

"Understandable all round." She put her napkin down and reached for her coffee, draining the last of it. Having someone cook for her was an unusual feeling. She quite liked it but felt a little uncomfortable that she was being managed and losing her independence. Realistically, Cassie knew this was what Babs did. It was her way of showering family and friends with love. Cassie was so used to looking out for herself and everyone around her, having someone else doing it for her was uncomfortable for her.

"I can see your mind churning over, sugar. What's going on in there?"

Cassie felt her cheeks heat. Caught out!

Babs laughed and leaned over to pat her hand. "Sugar, your face. Priceless, I tell you."

Cassie shrugged. "I'm feeling kinda guilty at being waited on if you must know." She tossed her bangs and tried to calm the embarrassment that statement brought up. She'd been independent for so long, it just felt wrong somehow.

"Well, you deal with it how you like, being the professional and all. For me, it's all about love and being generous to your fellow man. As much as I want to give you the world for what you've done for this family, this is what I do for anyone I meet. Understand?"

Daniel dropped his fork with a clatter on the plate and giggled.

Babs reached over and took it, putting it in the dishwasher under the counter. "Finished young man?"

He scrambled out of his chair and went around to hug his grandmother. She held him close and lifted tear filled eyes to Cassie.

Got it, Babs, enough said.

Babs cleared her throat and let go of Daniel. "Right, Daniel. How about we go down to Toby's house and see what he's got that you can borrow? I feel an crafty morning coming up, what do you say?"

He immediately glanced over at Cassie, "Can you come with me?" Apprehension clouded his eyes, and she was once again reminded of how much he needed her, how much he relied on her. There was no way she was going anywhere soon, and she may as well make the most of it. "I'm way overdue for a creative morning, Daniel. Let's go see what we can find, shall we?"

He grinned and clapped his hands. "Yes, yes!"

Together with Babs, they left the house and headed down toward the barn, taking the route to the little white cottage nestled between the horse pastures. Way beyond the pastures, a range of mountains tipped their peaks to the clear blue sky. Everything looked calm and serene with the animals slowly making their way from one patch of grass to the next without a care in the world. Chickens scratched in the yard, fluttering out of the way of horse's hooves. There was a serenity to the place that she hadn't felt before. And it wasn't just that she was somewhere safe. It was more than that. If she had been able to choose her perfect place to settle down, this ranch would come awfully close to top of her wish list.

How amazing would it be to live here without the fear that dogged her now. She couldn't imagine being somewhere where everything was peaceful and calm.

The air was crisp and clean, the sounds of animals and men working was melodic rather than the hectic bustle she was used to.

Daniel skipped ahead which gave the women time to chat quietly.

"Tell me what you're going to achieve, sugar. If you don't

want us to ask him questions, what are you hoping to get out of this art therapy?"

Cassie leaned down and picked a blade of grass before answering. "It's a way for Daniel to get the stress or anxiety of the episode out in a safe way that doesn't make him feel pressured. He's been having nightmares, the reason I still sleep with him. That's not going to get better unless he can find an outlet for his fear, and we can try to deal with it."

"Understood."

They came to the house and Babs opened the door. "Come on inside."

The cottage was tiny and so cutely furnished it looked like it belonged in a magazine shoot. The interior was painted white with pops of navy blue in the cushions on the oatmeal lounge chairs and in the curtains. The tiny kitchen was spotless. The only thing on the counters were the blue and white striped containers and the vase of silk flowers.

Cassie was used to the bare basics in her apartment. She never had time for the frills in life because she was so busy with work. But this place made her rethink what she wanted out of life. Being on the ranch had given her time to let her mind wander and ask herself the questions of 'what if?' What if she couldn't go back to work? What if she would never be able to go back out into the world like she had been? What if they didn't give up until they caught her?

Babs' voice broke into her thoughts. "Cora, Duke and Toby will be home in a few days. They're all so excited to meet you too. It took Daddy all types of smooth talking to stop them coming home early when they found out you'd arrived." Babs sighed. "Duke tends to overdo things in the restaurant, and it took Cora a long time to convince him to go away for a couple of weeks break. A bit like a delayed honeymoon that they both deserved."

"That's sweet. Are you sure they don't mind us being in here?" Cassie wasn't sure how she'd feel if someone walked into her house and helped themselves to her things, but truth be told, they probably already had. She imagined it trashed like Lissa's house and a shudder rolled down her back.

"Not at all. This family shares everything and we don't hold back as you probably already guessed. Cora already said to let Daniel have anything he wants. A lot of the things in here belonged to him when he was a baby anyway. Adam had it in storage and when Toby came along, we pulled it out to try and make him feel at home."

Cassie stared at Babs, waiting for the rest of the story.

"Cora was running from a bad domestic situation and Duke employed her to run his restaurant on the recommendation of a friend. Toby was a bonus and I love that boy. You will too."

"How old is he?"

"Going on eight now. He came here when he was about Daniel's age."

Cassie watched as Daniel wandered into Toby's bedroom and climbed up on the bed. She leaned on the door frame as he reached up to the little bookshelf. He pulled a book down and sat on the bed, legs tucked under himself and opened the book. His fingers traced the words, and he screwed his face up.

She waited patiently for him to say something, but he turned the pages quietly, his mouth working with silent words. When he came to the end of the book, he slammed it shut and held it to his chest.

"I bought him that when he was tiny." Babs' voice was a whisper as she leaned into Cassie. "He remembers it."

Cassie nodded. "He does." She waited to see if he would react. When he didn't, she stepped into the room.

"Toby said you can take anything you like, Daniel. Would you like to keep that book?"

He stared at her with serious eyes a moment before answering. "Mine. It's mine."

Babs sighed. "I bought you that book, Daniel because you like baby animals so much. You remember it."

He grinned at his grandmother and scrambled off the bed, handing it to her. "Please read to me."

Babs hiccupped a sob and wrapped her arm around his shoulders, guiding him out to the loungeroom where they sat in a big chair together. While Babs read the book, Cassie opened the wardrobe Bab's had pointed out and started collecting art supplies.

By the time Babs had finished reading, she had collected paper, paints, and crayons to take to the house.

"I think this is enough for now. Let's go paint, Daniel."

***

Adam rode back into the yard, shut the gate behind the steers he'd rounded up and slid from his horse, slipping the reins over its head so they didn't drag on the ground.

"That all of them, Adam?"

His father took his horse and led it into the wash bay.

"That's the last of them. Be good to ship them out. I want to take a good inventory of the stock we have left before we head into the next breeding cycle. That bull we were talking about, the one Reg Nichols is talking of selling?"

"What about him?"

"I'm having second thoughts. Tyler Fisher called me last night. He's bringing in some stock from up north and suggests we take a look before we make any decisions. Some pretty good genetics there or so he says. Be a good improvement to our beef if we have the opportunity. About time we brought in some new blood lines too."

His father slipped the saddle from his horse and handed it to Adam. "If you think it's a good idea, sure. Let's look at it."

Adam turned to walk the saddle into the tack room and stopped. His mother, Cassie and Daniel were walking out of Dukes little house. Mama saw him and waved. She leaned down and spoke to Daniel.

His son paused and glanced at Cassie before turning, Adam's heart doubled in size when he started running down toward him. Adam offloaded the saddle on a fence rail and walked toward his son, thrilled to see a smile on his face. At last, Daniel was getting more relaxed around him. So much had changed in the short time they'd been home.

"Hey, champ. What do you have there?" He crouched down as Daniel met him.

He held out a book, one that Adam remembered. "My book. Grandma read it to me."

He handed it to his father and Adam swallowed the emotion that crept up his throat. "I remember this one. It was your favorite story." He smiled and ruffled his son's hair. "Maybe we can read it tonight when you go to bed."

A shadow moved over them. "That's a great idea." Cassie smiled warmly at him. Backlit by the morning sun, Cassie appeared to glow. The golden light streaking through her hair, as a gentle breeze collected the long golden strands. God, she was stunning.

Adam stood as Daniel ran down to the barn and glanced at the art supplies she held close to her chest. "So, looks like you have something planned."

"Yes. I think it's time for some art therapy. Daniel can express himself through drawing or painting. It works really well." She glanced over his shoulder and her eyes went wide. "Is he okay?"

Adam followed her gaze, Daniel had slipped away and was stroking his horse as his grandfather walked it to the stall.

"He's fine. Always had a way with the animals, even as a tiny toddler. I thought he'd forgotten how much he loved them but obviously he hasn't."

"I often believe that kind of empathy is inbuilt into our DNA and can't be lost no matter what happens."

Adam scuffed the ground with his boot. "Has he said anything yet?" He wanted to help his son but with Cassie being the professional, he felt he had to follow her lead. And the connection she had with her son was one to be relied upon, not pushed to one side. Besides, he liked having her around to do this with him. He felt like he wasn't doing this alone. And that was something he always felt with Lissa, even when she was living with him as his wife.

That was the revelation that came to him a few nights ago. He hadn't looked at a woman for years. His whole focus had been to keep his sanity while trying to find his son. Romance was never going to get any headspace. Now though, things could be different, and he felt a twinge of hope burst into life in his chest.

Cassie shook her head, her blonde hair swaying with the sunlight catching the lighter strands. "Not a word." She watched Daniel interacting with his grandfather and a contented smile softened her features. "The worst thing we can do is push him to talk about what happened." She gave him a quick smile and looked back at his son. "Being there was traumatic for me so I can only imagine what it's done to Daniel. At least the nightmares aren't as bad as they were."

"Yes, that's a lot to be grateful for." He swallowed before

he spoke again. "As is having you here, Cassie. Look, I know I was angry when you arrived, and I promise you I wasn't mad at you. I'd almost given up hope of ever seeing Daniel again and there you were, cradling my son in your arms and...I just...I didn't know what to do. I'm sorry for the way I treated you then. I just didn't know what the heck had happened, and I was about to lose my mind."

She put a hand on his arm, and he covered it with his hand. "Don't beat yourself up over it, Adam. I totally get it. I would have reacted the same way if some stranger had come to my home with my missing child." She squeezed before removing her hand. "Let's just work together and do the best we can for Daniel. He deserves whatever happiness we can give him."

"What about you, Cassie?"

She glanced up at him and a dusting of pink washed her perfect cheekbones.

"I know this is hard on you, not being able to go home because it's not safe. I feel responsible for that and I'm sorry but I'm not sorry you're here."

"I'll do anything for Daniel." She held the supplies tight to her chest.

"I don't mean just for my son. I, um, I really like having you here too."

She lifted her head and stared at him, blinking rapidly, her mouth open.

Had he overstepped the mark?

12

Cassie sipped her coffee and watched Daniel working on his creation. Nothing so far had alerted her to the trauma he was keeping inside.

Babs worked quietly in the kitchen, making a big pot of chili for dinner that night and the smells made Cassie's mouth water.

"That smell reminds me of home, Babs. My mother is a great cook but it's my daddy who is the chili expert in the family."

Babs chuckled. "Just wait until you try mine, sugar and then tell me who has the best recipe."

Out of nowhere, Daniel's cries pierced the air and he threw his paintbrush at the wall.

"Daniel, what's wrong?" Cassie put her coffee down and stood but he swiped his hand across the table and sent the paint brush mug flying, the dirty water running down the wall in a rainbow of colors. Bab's gasped.

His face was twisted in anger and frustration. "I want my mom. You took me away from her." He screamed a primal roar and ran out of the house, the door slamming behind him.

"Sugar, we have to go after him." Babs wiped her hands on her apron and whipped it off as she started to the door.

Cassie grabbed her arm. "Give him a minute. He needs to vent and it's best if he does it on his own without us telling him how to feel and what to do." She wanted desperately to go after him, but she knew he needed space, even if it was only for a few minutes. "He's safe here, Babs. You keep telling me that."

Babs sighed and wrung her hands. "Yes, but he's just a little boy."

"He's a little boy that has suffered a very big trauma. We're doing what's best for him, I promise. I'm sure he's just out on the porch, we can go out and see if he's okay. I suspect he will be ready for a hug right about now."

The relief in Babs eyes was plain to see. "Let's go."

Cassie followed her outside and glanced around. No sign of him on the porch or in the yard.

"You go to the back of the house, and I'll go out the front. He's probably down at the barn with grandpa." Babs gave her a gentle shove and took off to the front of the house.

Cassie hurried around the back, calling Daniel as she went. But as she passed the front door and ducked her head to check under the front porch and he wasn't there, an uneasy feeling clutched at her stomach.

"Daniel, Daniel, come out babe. It's okay. No one is mad at you." Silence met her statement.

She hurried down the side of the house to where Babs was standing with her hands on her hips, a worried frown on her face.

"Sugar, I'm nervous. Let's hurry down to the barn. Someone is bound to have seen him." She turned and scurried down the drive, calling out to the men lingering around the wash bay and the older man with his head under the hood of a truck. He lifted his head out and wiped his brow with a stained bandana. "What's up Ma'am?"

"Y'all seen our Daniel? Anyone?"

"Been out here for the last half hour working on this old thing and ain't seen no boy come this way." He tipped his chin at the men washing horses. "You seen a young'un around?"

They both shook their heads and went back to what they were doing.

Cassie grabbed Babs' arm as the panic started to show on her face. "Come inside the barn and check it out. He loves it down here."

Babs turned a fear-filled face to her and Cassie's heart almost broke. Babs and the rest of the family had been through so much when Daniel had first disappeared. Her emotional reaction is not just understandable, but expected.

"He'll be here somewhre. He's hurting, Babs and is having trouble processing that. Come on, stay strong for me." She guided her inside the huge barn.

It took a few minutes for her sight to adjust to the dust and darkness. "This way." She headed to where Daniel found the eggs the first day he was down here. He'd scampered up the hay bales, chortling in glee as he tumbled back down before discovering the hidden nest tucked behind the huge pile.

"Ladies. Aren't you a sight for sore eyes." Grandpa was leaning over a fence railing rubbing the head of a tan calf that was attempting to suck on his fingers. Its tongue curled around his fingers as he scratched its head.

"Daddy, have you seen Daniel?" Babs' voice was wavering with emotion.

"Adam said he was up with you doing some painting therapy." Grandpa wiped his hand on the back of his denim jeans and reached out to his daughter-in-law, wrapping a steady arm around her shoulders.

"We were. He got upset about his mama and took off. We gave him a few minutes before we went out to see him and now, we can't find him."

"Crap!" Grandpa strode through the barn over to the open back double doors and whistled loudly, making Cassie's ears ring. He waved his arms and called Adam's name. Cassie chewed on her lip, Babs nervousness starting to rub off on her. Had she made the right decision giving Daniel space? She'd thought so, but now the what-if's were racing through her head. Her stomach twisted as Adam marched towards the barn.

Cassie couldn't stand still waiting for what she thought would be a dressing down from Adam, so she walked around the barn, looking behind equipment and inside stalls to try and find Daniel while Grandpa called in reinforcements.

She didn't know if she could deal with anyone else freaking out like Babs right now. Adam blaming her for Daniel's outburst crossed her mind. Had she pushed him too soon? It was easy to make a wrong judgment with childhood trauma, especially in cases such as this. She'd been so focused on getting them to safety, she hadn't really thought as clearly as she should have until they were safe. His trauma could easily have manifested in a bigger way than she'd expected.

Now she needed a clear head to help her find Daniel before he was hurt. This ranch was huge and she hadn't considered that when she said to give him space. She stared out at the mountains. He could be anywhere.

"Cassie. What the heck?" Adam grabbed her arm, anguish clear on his face.

"He can't be far away, Adam. He was upset."

"Why?"

She looked at the hand gripping her arm too tight and then his face. He let her go.

"Sorry, Cassie. It's... I mean, I'm having trouble not thinking the worst, you know?"

She tried to smile reassuringly at him, but it was strained. In her gut she had the same feeling Adam did and she was supposed to be looking after Daniel getting him assimilated to being back home and she'd failed in probably the most awful way. By losing him if only for a short time. She could hardly blame him for being upset at her.

"I understand why you're upset, Adam but you have to try and put yourself in his position. He's been through a lot and the only thing that was constant for those last few years was his mom, even if she wasn't the best person for him to be with. His outburst showed me he knows she's missing, and he's scared for her. Maybe he saw her taken, I have no idea, but we have to presume the worst has happened to her." It made her feel ill wondering if Daniel saw her assaulted and possibly murdered.

"And he's probably thinking the same, is that what you're thinking?"

Cassie sighed wishing it was easier. "Yeah, I would if I was in his shoes. He may be upset we haven't looked for her. He doesn't know how to process what he's been through." And that was why she was there. To help him. Look what a great job she was doing so far.

Adam shook his head and looked everywhere but at Cassie. "Hell."

"Yeah. So, we need to find him and assure him that the

authorities are doing everything they can to find her and it's our job to keep him safe in the meantime."

∼

He thought for a moment. "Clay. I'll call Clay and he can come and have a chat to Daniel in a way he would understand."

Cassie sighed, wrapping her arms across her stomach. She seemed so vulnerable in that moment and he wanted to hold her close, reassure her everything was going to be okay. She was doing more than anyone had a right to expect after what she got caught up in. In the end he gave up and put his arm around her shoulders, his heart racing when she leaned into him. Together they would sort this out, he was sure of it.

"Don't blame yourself, Cassie. I used to storm off when I got into trouble from Mama too and Daniel probably can't deal right now. We'll find him."

She glanced into his face, her eyes troubled with just a hint of tears. Her lip wobbled. "It's my fault, Adam. I should have seen this outburst coming." She wiped her hands over her face and took a quick intake of breath. "Some therapist I am. I can't believe you want me to stay here. I'm failing Daniel and you, in more ways than one."

He pulled her around so they were facing each other and gripped her shoulders, leaning down so they were so close he could feel her breath on his face. "Don't talk like that. If it wasn't for you, Daniel could well be dead by now or smuggled away to goodness knows what kind of place." He cupped her cheeks with his hands, wiping the solitary tear that slid down her cheek with his work roughened thumb. "If it wasn't for you, I would never have gotten my son back."

She closed her eyes and a tremble ran though her body. Her mouth opened but no sound came out.

"Cassie, honey, it's okay, I promise. He's a little boy with issues that will take time to deal with. Plus, he probably has his father's temper. He'll be hiding somewhere safe. I promise you we will find him."

She pressed herself against his chest and sobbed. He figured it was probably the tension she'd been holding in since she'd arrived. She'd remained calm and slightly distant but had never given into the fear she must have been feeling apart from the nightmares.

She took a few deep breaths and pushed herself away from him. He kept a steadying hand on her arm while she pulled herself together.

"Want to walk around and see if you can help me find him?"

Cassie gave him a watery smile and nodded. "Yes, thanks."

He took her hand and steered her back to where Babs and Grandpa stood.

Babs looked at Cassie with her heart in her eyes. "It's okay, Mama, I'll walk with Cassie and you go with Grandpa and focus on the barn and surrounding yards. We'll head back toward the house and check the cottages and men's quarters. There are a few places I know he could be hiding in."

Mama patted Cassie on the arm and walked with Grandpa inside the barn.

"I'm sorry I lost it. I don't usually let my emotions get the better of me like that."

Adam smiled. "You deserve to lose it as you put it. I can't believe how strong you've been through all of this."

Cassie gave a short laugh. "What's that saying? You don't

know how strong you are until you have to be? I never imagined it would be anything like this, you know. More like I'd have a patient I couldn't connect with. That was my biggest fear. Or at least it used to be."

"And now?"

"That they come looking for me and Daniel."

That was Adam's biggest fear now too.

13

Adam held her hand as they walked away from the barn. "See that old falling down shed behind the white cottage? That was a favorite place of mine when I was growing up. It's probably dangerous and full of spiders and think it's the only reason I haven't turned it into a bonfire. It holds so many memories."

"Daniel wouldn't....

"If he's anything like I was growing up, he would. When a young boy gets emotional or upset, he doesn't think straight. I'm sure you know all this and as much as I don't like to admit it, I was that kind of child. I don't know how Mama put up with me. I was the family drama queen until I hit my tenth birthday when suddenly the world didn't seem so big and scary to me." He squeezed her hand and kept talking. "My father had so much patience, I just wish I was the same way but I'm not the most tolerant person these days." He knew why but had never given it much voice.

Cassie leaned into him as they walked over the pasture to the dilapidated shed. Adam pulled her into the doorway, waiting for his eyes to adjust to the shadows.

"I'll wait here if you don't mind." Cassie let go of his hand and wrapped her arms around herself, it made her look young and vulnerable.

"Sure. This will only take a minute." He strode over to the old rusted out tractor and crouched down to look underneath it. The feed grain sacks were still where he'd left them, more dust now than hessian. But no Daniel. He did a quick scout around the shed, checking behind bundles of timber stacked for future use and then forgotten. No sign of his son.

"He's not here. Let's do a scout around the cottages and the men's quarters before I show you my favorite hiding places around the main house. But you have to promise not to tell anyone." He cupped his hand under her chin and lifted it, so she was staring him in the eyes. Poor girl was taking this very seriously. It was a shame she was so determined to blame herself for what Adam would just call a childish fit of temper. He knew nothing would hurt his son on this ranch.

He knew every inch of the property and every single person that worked here. Daniel was safe.

"Try not to worry so much, Cassie. He's just being a normal kid who is struggling with his emotions and that's understandable. He has us to lean on, to help him through. It will be fine. I promise."

She blinked and he was struck at how pretty the golden flecks in her hazel eyes were with her standing in the sun. "I can't help but worry. We need to find him, Adam."

"I know. Let's go." He took her hand and led her to the first cottage. It didn't take them long to figure out he wasn't in the empty building. They moved onto Duke's place.

As soon as they walked in, Adam heard the soft crying from his boy.

Cassie pointed to the bedroom where they'd found the art and craft earlier. Together they crept in and saw Daniel huddled on the bed with a big stuffed dog crushed in his arms. She moved over and sat down on the edge of the bed, reaching out to him. "Daniel."

She touched his back, and he tensed before turning a tear-stained face toward her.

"It's okay, Daniel. It's okay." She rubbed his back as Adam leaned over and scooped up his son. He looked so small cradled against Adam's big, broad chest and her mind went back to the last few nights when she'd run to him when the nightmare had her bolting from her bed. He'd held her while she shook with fear, soothing her just like he was calming Daniel. Funny how she felt safe with him and didn't hesitate to reach out when she needed him. She'd even fallen asleep wrapped in his arms, waking to find herself back in her own bed in the morning. She shook off the memory and focused on Daniel and Adam.

He sat on the bed next to Cassie and she didn't hesitate to snuggle in close, wrapping her arm around Daniel, together they hugged the sad little boy.

After a few minutes the tears ceased, and Daniel wriggled in his father's arms.

He stared at Cassie, his lip trembling. "Are you mad at me?"

She wiped a tear from his cheek with her finger. "No, honey. I'm not mad in the slightest. You have lots of big feelings going on and I'm here to help you manage that."

Adam kissed him on the head and held him close. "Buddy, nothing you do is going to make us angry at you. Understand that, okay?"

"Yes, Daddy." He snuggled against his father's chest and reached for Cassie's hand. "They hurt mama." He stared at Cassie, his big blue eyes troubled.

"I know, honey." Her heart hurt for the little boy.

"I ran away. I got scared." He sniffed and wiped his nose with the back of his hand.

"You had every right to be scared, Daniel. I was scared too." Cassie struggled to keep her voice even as the memories came back. She swallowed and took a breath. "You were very brave."

He shook his head. "No, I wasn't."

Adam stared at Cassie as he spoke. "You were brave, Daniel. Your mama wouldn't have wanted you to get hurt. You did the right thing."

Daniel turned his face up to his father and a tear slid down his face. "Is she dead? Is my mama dead?"

A hand clutched Cassie's heart and squeezed. "I hope not, Daniel. Your Uncle Clay is doing the best he can to find out what happened."

Daniel stared at her again. "He wasn't there." He chewed on his lip.

"No, he wasn't. It was just you and then me." Cassie held her breath.

"The bad man hit her, and I ran away." He looked at the stuffed animal he'd been holding. "Can I tell him? Will it help him help mommy?" He glanced up at his father.

Adam shared a glance with Cassie, and she gave a small nod. "If that's what you want to do, sure. We can go up to the house and call him. Grandma will make you cookies and milk too while we wait. What do you say?"

Daniel struggled out of his father's hands, put the stuffed animal back where he found it and scurried off the bed.

They followed him out of the cottage. Adam turned down to the barn and gave a loud whistle. Grandpa came running out and they exchanged hand signals.

"How did you make that noise with your mouth, Daddy?" Daniel touched his cheek and Adam melted.

Adam pushed back the emotion in his throat and grinned. "Want me to teach you how to whistle?"

Daniel grinned and nodded his head.

"How about we do that this afternoon after lunch." He was too emotional to try now. Tears threatened and he didn't want to embarrass himself.

Daniel wrapped his arm around Adam's neck and tried blowing his own whistle, but the noise was more like a wet raspberry landing on the floor. Adam stifled a smile.

"Let's go. Mama will be up as soon as she hears the news." Adam slipped his arm around her shoulders and Cassie felt more at peace than she had in ages. He was right. Daniel hadn't gone far, and it seemed they were making progress with the art therapy after all. It got him talking and that was hopefully going to help them find out what happened to Daniel's mother.

14

"Cookies. My favorite." Clay sat next to Daniel at the kitchen island and reached for the plate, dragging it over so they could both reach it.

Cassie and Adam sat at the small breakfast table giving Clay the okay to do it his way, but she would be ready to step in if she thought anything was being counterproductive or detrimental to Daniels wellbeing.

Clay took a bite and took his time chewing, letting Daniel get used to him being there. "Your daddy tells me you were very brave, Daniel. I'm proud of you."

Daniel shook his head. "I ran away. That's not brave."

Clay swallowed the last piece of cookie and wiped his hands. "Now that's where you're wrong. If it stops you being hurt, that's an act of bravery in my books."

Daniel stared at Clay, his eyes wide.

"Trust me. I know these things. I'm the sheriff and it's my job to keep people safe. If I'd been there, I would have told you to run."

Daniel stared at him in wonder. "You would?"

"Of course I would. He was a big bad man, and he was

being mean to your mom. It would have been silly for you to stay there and get hurt, don't you think?"

Daniel glanced over at Cassie. She smiled at him.

"I guess." He fiddled with the hem of his t-shirt before glancing back at Clay. "Can you find my mama?"

Cassie held her breath and Adam reached for her hand. Was this the breakthrough in the case they needed?

∼

ADAM mentally crossed everything that Daniel wouldn't get too scared to share what he knew with Clay.

Of course he was angry at Lissa for stealing his son and keeping them apart for the last three years. Yes, he was furious that she was involved in drugs again and put their son at risk. But still, he wanted her to be safe more than anything. If Daniel could give Clay enough information they might be able to find her.

"Well, I can do my best but that would mean you telling me what happened on that day." Clay kept his voice low and calm, and Adam thanked God that his brother wasn't the type to get rattled easily. It was what made him a great sheriff.

"Everything?" Daniel stared at Cassie, worry creasing his forehead.

Cassie rose and moved over to crouch beside him. "Daniel, nothing can hurt you here. I promise you that and I will be with you every step of the way."

Daniel grabbed her hand and stared at him. "Daddy?"

Adam rose and hurried to his son, picking him up and holding him close to his chest. "I've got you, son. I'm not going anywhere, and nobody is going to hurt you."

Mama spoke, breaking the emotional tension filling the

kitchen. "How about y'all go into the loungeroom. Grandpa lit the fire earlier because the chill was making his bones ache he said. I'll bring in the cookies and make some hot chocolate, might help y'all relax more. How does that sound?"

"Perfect, Mama. Thank you." Adam dropped a kiss on his son's head. "I don't know about you, little buddy, but I feel the need for a nice big mug of my Mama's frothy hot chocolate in front of the fire. You with me?"

Daniel giggled and wriggled against him as Adam tickled him in the ribs. "Yes!"

Together they walked to the front loungeroom, and Adam sat on the big leather couch with Daniel beside him and Cassie on the other side.

Clay took the chair opposite and crossed his leg, leaning back into the soft buttery leather. "I love sitting here. It's like we're in another world."

Mama walked in with a tray bearing mugs of hot chocolate and Clay jumped up to help her. He shared the mugs out, placing them on the table in front of the couch.

"Babs, if you could join us, please. I think Daniel would benefit with all those he loves around him right now." Cassie patted the arm of the chair next to them.

She sat and pushed the plate of cookies toward Daniel. "Made fresh this morning. Double chocolate chip."

Clay reached over and snatched a couple before anyone could stop him. Mama slapped at his hand, and he squealed making Daniel laugh.

Adam shared a glance over Daniel's head with Cassie and gave him a slight nod. Whatever Daniel shared affected them both, but Adam knew Cassie's main concern was for his welfare and for that, he would be forever grateful. Would telling them upset him again and send him to a darker place than he was now or would it free him to share what had happened? Would it be something that would put them all on edge more than they were already? He could see Cassie was nervous waiting for his words.

Adam reached over and gripped her hand, giving it a squeeze. His message was clear. They would get through this as a family.

15

"In your own time, Daniel. Just tell me what happened, okay?"

Daniel wiped his hand across his mouth, brushing away the crumbs from the second cookie he'd consumed. "Mama was angry with me." He frowned. "I didn't do anything. I told her that, but she yelled at me anyway."

Adam rubbed his hand over his son's back, working it in circles.

Clay leaned forward in his chair. "Did she tell you why?"

Daniel shook his head.

"What happened then, Daniel?"

"That man came in his big truck." He shivered and Adam glanced at Cassie. She held Daniel's hand. "He smiled at me with yucky shiny teeth."

Clay nodded. "I have a photo here. If I show you a photo, could you tell me if it was him?"

Daniel shrugged.

Clay opened the file on the table in front of them and

held up the rap sheet with the leader of the cartel's photo on it.

Daniel stared at it for a moment and then dropped his head, giving a sigh.

"Was that him, Daniel?"

"Uh huh."

"What happened then?"

"Mama told me to go outside but there was another man at the door, and he scared me, so I took Ted and went and hid behind the couch."

Ted, the only thing that he had that belonged to him. The dirty stuffed bear that he slept with most nights. His only connection with the last few years that had come with him when they ran. Adam had asked his mother to wash it but so far, Daniel wasn't letting anyone touch it. Cassie had assured him it was in Daniel's best interests to have control over his toy.

"And then what happened?" Clay put the rap sheet upside down on the table.

"They screamed at each other." Daniel leaned into Adam. "It made my ears hurt."

"I bet it did. Adults can really yell loud, can't they. I wonder what they were mad at?" Clay looked pensive as if he was trying to figure out and Adam gave him points for being so kind to his son.

Daniel sat up, his eyes lighting up. "Money. He yelled at Mama because she kept his money, and he was really mad. Like, he broke glasses on the counter and everything." The fear was no longer radiating from Daniel. Now it was more excitement as he shared what happened.

"Could you see them from your spot in the living room?"

Daniel nodded fast. "Yeah, I sure could. Ted and I were sitting on the floor behind the couch near the front door, and I could see Mama through the other door. She kept hitting him and telling him off. She said he didn't know how good he had it or something. Said she worked hard for him and then he hit her." Daniel huddled against Adam. "Real hard across the face. She said a bad word to him, called him names."

"It's okay, son. I've got you. He can't hurt you here. We have Grandpa, Clay and all the men on the ranch to take care of us."

His son looked up at him with huge eyes. "But he had a big knife, Daddy. Like, huge." He held out his arms to show the length of the weapon.

"That's some knife." Clay sipped his hot chocolate, licked his lips and put it down again. "Did you get marshmallows in yours, Daniel?"

Daniel opened his mouth to speak and then leaned forward, looking in his cup. When he discovered the soft pillowy sweets, he grinned. "Yay!" He dipped his finger in and pulled it out with melted marshmallow dripping down his hand as he slurped it up, smearing it over his lips.

***

Cassie mouthed a thank you to Clay. He was doing so well interviewing Daniel that the reluctance she felt initially when he'd arrived faded away.

Adam leaned over and rubbed her shoulder behind Daniel's back. "You okay?"

"Perfect, thank you." She was as keen as they were to find out what happened before she'd arrived on scene but she'd been worried about how Daniel would handle it.

The next few minutes were going to be the most traumatic if she was correct. Steering Daniel through them would take the adults to be calm and reassuring.

Daniel finished licking his fingers and stared at Clay

again as if he'd remembered why he was here. "He was still real mad at her cause she screamed really loud, and I hid behind the couch and covered my face with Ted. When everything went quiet, I peeked. I saw blood on the kitchen wall."

Cassie put a reassuring hand on Daniel's leg, holding her breath.

"Wow, that must have frightened you." Clay's voice was soft as it had been all through the interview. "What did you do then?"

"Mama yelled at me to run but I was scared."

Adam put his hand around Daniel's shoulders. "You're the bravest little boy I know."

Daniel stared up at his father before speaking again. "She kept screaming at me and then the bad man outside the kitchen came in and grabbed her. He pushed her against the wall and then the other man with the knife looked at me funny. It made me scared, so Ted and me ran out the front door and hid, just like Mama told me too. I didn't come out till the bad men drove away in the truck." He sighed. "And then Cassie came and put me in her car."

"You did the right thing, Daniel."

"Can you find my mama?"

"I'm going to do the best I can, that I promise."

"Okay." Daniel finished his hot chocolate and snuggled into his father. "I'm tired, Daddy." His shoulders slumped and he yawned.

Babs stood. "Let me take you up for a little rest before lunch, Daniel. I can read you a story if you like." She held out her hand and he grinned up at her. "Some memories are enough to make a body tired."

"Two stories, Grandma?"

Babs laughed. "Just like your daddy trying to push the limits. We will see."

Once they were out of sight, Clay sighed. "That went better than I expected."

"I'm so grateful Daniel ran when his mother told him to." Cassie rubbed her hands over her face. "But getting back to then. When I arrived, both Daniel's mom and the cartel leader had disappeared and only that creep Raoul searching the house was there. The question is, did he take her, or did she manage to get away from him?"

Clay stood. "I can reach out to my counterparts in that area and tell them what we know but realistically, I don't like our chances of finding her alive. Not if she's mixed up with that crew. Anyone crosses them, they disappear never to be seen again."

Cassie felt a niggle deep in her gut. "What are we supposed to do in the meantime?" She rubbed her hands up her arms. "I'm sick of hiding from them already."

Adam turned to her and put his hands on her arms, staring into her eyes. "You need to stay here where we can keep an eye on you, Cassie. Those men are dangerous, and you can identify them. You won't be safe until they're locked up."

She glanced over at Clay. "Why would they bother looking for us. In the scheme of things, Daniel and I are just another annoyance they probably don't really care about. It was her they were after and even if I can identify them, I hardly think that will worry them." She took a deep breath. "Realistically, what are the chances of you catching them and making charges stick?"

He shrugged. "Not my case at the end of the day. I'm merely feeding the powers that be the information but with the FBI involved, which they should be by now, I think we stand a better chance of seeing them behind bars eventually. It's not like they hide their operation, is it? They think they're invincible and enough people are scared of them to let them get away with it. Probably why they haven't even bothered to look for you and Daniel yet."

"You can't know that, Clay. For all we know, they could already be in town." Adam sounded more worried than Clay.

"You're right, I don't know that for sure. But if they were trying to track Cassie down, I think we would have heard from the hotels or gas station where Cassie used her credit card. So far, local law enforcement has reported nothing unusual." Adam didn't seem convinced.

And when his eyes met Cassie's, they were filled with concern.

16

Adam put his arms around Cassie's shoulders and tucked her into his side as if it was the most natural thing in the world to do. "I'm not prepared to take any chances. Not with you or my son." A weird warmth pooled in her belly, making her very aware of how his hand skimmed down her back and settled on the side of her waist. His thumb traced small circles, grazing the strip of exposed skin just above the waistband of her jeans, where her borrowed top sat a little short and snug. Her heart skipped in her chest and heat crept its way up her neck. She hoped her reaction to him wasn't obvious to anyone around them.

Clay smiled. "Better listen to my brother, Cassie. He's a hard man to argue with."

She leaned against the hard chest and wondered what had come over her. Was she falling for the brooding cowboy? The thought scared the heck out of her. Maybe it was the circumstances, and it was her brains way of coping. Wanting someone so soon after meeting them wasn't right nor did it make sense. From the nights he'd held her when she had nightmares to the support he gave her when she messed up with Daniel. But right now she needed to focus on Clay and what he's saying.

"Do you think it would be okay for me to go to town and get a coffee and watch the people walk by. I just feel like I'm sequestered or something."

Adam snorted and she wanted to elbow him in the gut. "I can think of worse places to be."

She spun around. "So can I and I don't mean that to sound derogatory or ungrateful because your family has been amazing to me. It's just that, this is me. I'm never not working. I'm always on the go with visits and calls to clients. I kinda feel like a prisoner in a very pretty setting, if you know what I mean."

Clay picked up his file and tucked it under one arm. "Can you call any of your clients from here without letting them know where you are? That way you can ease your mind over not being able to be there and keep safe at the same time."

"I probably could." She frowned. "There're a couple of clients I really should make contact with. I'm sure my boss will help out if she needs to but I know them better than anyone else and they do rely on me."

Adam pointed at the telephone on the side table. "Use that, the number is blocked and silent, so it won't show up on any caller ID's. Make as many calls as necessary. Just stay safe, is all I'm asking."

Cassie nodded. It was the best she was going to get.

∼

"Brother, be careful with her, won't you?" Clay opened the car door and stood staring at his brother.

Adam scowled at him. "I don't know what you're talking about."

Clay sighed. "Don't be stupid. You know exactly what I'm talking about. Cassie. How you feel about her. I can see it in your eyes. Just go easy on her is all I'm saying. She came into this by pure chance and once things are sorted out, you might not be able to keep her here. Don't set yourself up to fail."

Heck, I didn't know my attraction to Cassie was so obvious. If Clay noticed, I bet everyone else has too. "Get out of here and stop being a nosy old woman." He tipped his hat to his brother and turned away.

But Clay wasn't finished with him yet. He followed him down the driveway, grabbing his arm. "Look, I know what it's like, but this is unusual circumstances to fall in love."

Adam spun around. "Who said I'm in love?"

Clay stood with his hands on his hips. "Are you serious? You know the reputation this family has for falling in love fast. I can see it in the way you watch her and touch her, bro. If you're not in love with her yet, you will be soon if you keep this up. It's obvious you have feelings for her."

"So what if I do? It's none of your business."

"Oh man, give up. You had plenty to say when Kate came back to town, so I get to give you my opinion too. Look, I just don't want you to get hurt. And I don't want you to hurt her either. She's a good person. Look how she put herself in danger for Daniel."

Adams gut warred with his heart. This wasn't gratitude being confused with love. He'd had time to get to know her when they had quiet times together at night. He knew what he was feeling. Trying to explain it to anyone, including his well-meaning brother was hard. He wouldn't understand.

"Just because you loved Kate all your life, doesn't make you an expert in all things heart related, brother."

"No. it doesn't. But I know you and the extra degrees I have in humanities and communications gives me more insight than you'll ever have. I study people, Adam. It's part of my job. And having Cassie here, saving your son, it's easy to confuse love and attraction with gratitude. That would really hurt a person like Cassie who thinks of everyone before she thinks of herself."

Adam stared over Clay's head at the horses with foals in the pasture behind the cottages. "I'm not getting the two confused. Truth is, I like her a lot more than I thought I would. I wanted to hate her at first, when she came here with Daniel because I didn't know what she'd risked to save him."

"Understandable."

"And then I started to get to know her. You know Mama made me sleep up at the house so I would be close to Daniel? Well, seems he's not the only one who is having nightmares about this whole thing."

Clay tilted his head. "Cassie?"

"Yeah. Most nights I end up going in and soothing her. It's a strange feeling having a woman in my arms again. At first it was just about me wanting to soothe her; after everything she did to bring Daniel home, but it quickly changed for me, Clay. It's more than that, it's…I don't know how to explain it. I want to have her close, to protect her, you know?"

Clay nodded.

"But it's more than that. She's a genuine person, it just feels easy with her. She doesn't always wake up with her nightmares, sometimes she just clings to me and settles right back down to sleep and hardly knows I've been there."

He scuffed the ground with his boot. "She and I talk a little bit if she wakes up. We're getting to know each other, and I've missed that. Ever since Lissa took off with Daniel, dating has been the last thing on my mind. Now I really want to take that step again with Cassie."

"I get it, Adam. But once this is all over and done with, will there be anything between the two of you? Relationships built on two people being thrown together like this isn't something that lasts, in my experience. I just don't want to see either of you hurt."

Adam glanced at him. "Well, how about you help me out then instead of fussing over it going wrong. Why not invite us to dinner with you and Kate. Give us some normal instead of Cassie being in fight or flight mode all the time."

Clay grinned. "Now that I can get behind. I'll talk to my dear wife and call you later."

A warmth crept up Adams chest. He was actually doing this, making the effort to build a relationship with Cassie?

Now all he had to do was convince her it was what he really wanted and how great they could be together and not because she was handy and taking care of his son. That thought had crossed his mind when he first had feelings as he held her in his arms when she had her nightmares.

Now he knew different, but he suspected she would need to be convinced. It was a lot to wrap her head around. Adam felt for her because her life had changed in the blink of an eye and he wanted to change it up even more.

But the first thing he needed to do was convince her to go on a double date with him.

That's the easy part...hopefully.

17

"Seriously, Adam?" He wanted to take her out to dinner. Why did she find that so hard to believe.

Adam pressed his lips together and stared at her. "I just thought it would be nice for us to go out and get away from this." He spread his arms. "If only for an evening. We can pretend we're normal."

Of course, Cassie felt comfortable around him. He'd been there for her ever since she'd arrived with Daniel. But that didn't mean they should be acting like this was a date. Maybe it wasn't. Maybe it was a thank you for almost losing your life saving my son, kind of dinner.

"I can see your mind overthinking." Adam grinned and she felt that familiar punch to the gut that seemed to be getting more and more common. "I like you, Cassie. Like, really like you and this is my chance to get to know you a little bit better in an adult situation. Kate is lovely and she really thought it would be nice to go out as a couple."

"I don't have anything to wear." So far she'd been wearing his sister's casual clothing around the house and that was fine but going out in them wouldn't feel right.

Adam grinned triumphantly, he knew he was winning her over. "Go through Ella's closet. She would be the first one to tell you to help yourself. She has way too many clothes that have never been worn. I'm sure there will be something in there that you'll like."

"Like? She has amazing taste." She tucked a strand of hair behind her ear and glanced at him. "So, this is really a date-night kind of date? Not a thank you, dinner? I just want to be clear from the start." She was blabbing but couldn't stop it. "I don't want any misunderstandings between us." She chewed her bottom lip and Adam's eye zeroed in on her mouth.

Adam stepped in close, his hand coming up to cup her jaw. She sucked in a breath as he dropped a soft kiss on her lips, taking his time. He hovered there for a moment, gently brushing his lips over hers once, twice. Her hands came up to grip the front of his shirt and she almost swooned against him.

When he moved back, she swayed and steadied herself against his chest. "Well, guess that answer is clear then." Her words came out breathily.

He grinned and reached for his hat. "I don't waste words and I will never lead you on, Cassie. I'm dead serious about wanting to get to know you more. You already have my thanks and will have them for the rest of my life. This is a me and you thing."

"Right." She glanced at her apple watch and mentally prepared for what she needed to do before being date worthy. First thing on the list was a nice, hot bath. It'd been ages since she'd soaked and primped for a date. A little jolt of excitement went through her. "Well, thank you. I'd love to go out to dinner." She wanted to tell him she'd like to get to know him better too, but something stopped her from saying the words aloud. Was it because she still felt they were in danger or was it because she didn't fully trust her emotions after what they'd been through.

Cassie of all people knew that an experience like this could make a person feel things they normally wouldn't feel and for her own benefit, she wanted to explore that more before committing to a relationship.

After all, she had a life somewhere else to deal with.

Or did she?

∼

"Mama, can you babysit tonight? Clay has asked Cassie and I out for a meal."

Babs clapped her hands. "Oh, Adam, I was so hoping you would see she was perfect for you."

He laughed and held up a hand in protest. "Dinner, Mama, nothing else. Chill out please and don't scare her off."

She clasped her hands over her chest. "Things will work out exactly like they're supposed to. I know they will."

She grinned and Adam knew he was talking for the sake of it. Mama had her way and there was no stopping her.

"I'd better go make sure she helps herself to Ella's wardrobe. That poor child has been recycling the same few outfits since she's been here no matter how often I tell her to help herself." She headed out of the kitchen toward the stairs and Adam watched her go, grinning to himself.

He had work to do before he stopped for the day. He headed back down to the stockyards where his father was sorting through the yearlings. Daniel was perched up on the top rail of the fence with Grandpa beside him watching.

"That little roan pony, Daniel, is gonna make a great little cutting horse one day, you mark my words."

Adam jumped up beside them. "I agree. She's one I earmarked earlier. Just want to see what Daddy thinks." He watched as she was funneled into the yard with another couple that his father had said he wanted. The horses they didn't keep for the ranch would be sold off at the end of the month at the local horse auctions.

"Daniel, are you okay to stay with Grandma tonight if I go out?" He held his breath as his son looked at him. "Cassie is coming with me."

Grandpa coughed and didn't look at him. "Boy will be fine, won't you, Daniel?"

Daniel screwed up his nose. "Can I come too?"

Adam shook his head, not looking into his son's pleading eyes. "Not this time. I think Cassie needs a night away after everything she's done. Don't you agree?"

Daniel shrugged. "I guess so."

"Thank you. Grandpa will read you a story, won't you Grandpa?"

The old man chuckled. "You can count on it."

"Promise you'll come back?"

"You know I will, buddy. I wouldn't leave you for the world."

It wasn't until he was getting ready later that afternoon that the butterflies started in his stomach. He hadn't been on a date in years and suddenly he felt like a teenager again. He gave himself a talking too and reached for his aftershave. As he splashed some into his hands and dabbed it on his cheeks, he cursed the trepidation pooling in his stomach. He couldn't afford to mess this up and he felt like he was walking a knifes edge trying to keep her safe as well as trying to form a relationship.

Perhaps it would have been better to wait but his heart wouldn't hear of it. Once again, he was reminded of the family reputation of falling in love faster than normal. He didn't quite believe it would happen to him after the way his last relationship had turned out. He thought he was going to go into old age on his own.

Adam stepped out of his bedroom, closing the door behind him just as Cassie walked out of her room. The soft hint of perfume hit his nose. Rose and vanilla.

She wore a buttery soft dress that clung to her curves and then fell like a waterfall to her knees. Her shoulders were bare apart from the floral wrap carelessly draped over them and the effect was stunning.

His mouth opened and he had to concentrate to close it. "You look… gorgeous, Cassie."

She blushed and lowered her eyes. "Thank you. Your mother was very generous letting me raid Ella's wardrobe. I feel a bit guilty."

He stepped forward and took her hand. "Don't, please. She would tell you anything you want is yours. I'll get her to call in and see you if it will make you feel any better."

Cassie glanced at him, a smile curving her lips. "Don't put her on the spot for me, please. That will make me feel even worse."

He felt the smoothness of her hands in his. "She'd love to meet you anyway. I know she would." He stared into her eyes and his heart thumped. Before he could stop himself and question his thoughts, he leaned down and covered her mouth with his.

Cassie sucked in a breath and wrapped her free hand around his neck, holding him close. Adam lost himself in the softness of her lips until a giggle made him pull away.

Daniel was clutching his old teddy watching them.

Cassie recovered first. "Have you had dinner, Daniel?"

Adam put an arm around her shoulders. "Does Grandma know where you are?"

Just then they heard Babs calling him and he turned and ran down the stairs.

"Let's go." Adam grabbed Cassie's hand and guided her down the stairs.

18

Cassie held her hands over her stomach. "That was pretty special. I'm so full." When the plate of ribs arrived, she'd protested that she would never do it justice. They'd all laughed and now she knew why. Once she tasted them, she couldn't stop until her plate was empty.

Kate laughed and picked up her glass. "Did you know that recipe is from Babs? That's the reason Duke started the restaurant. His mom is a terrific cook, and he wanted to share that with the world."

"Oh, I know. She's been feeding me up."

"That's mama for you." Clay picked up his beer and took a sip before talking again. "Starting to feel a bit more relaxed leaving the safety of the ranch now, Cassie?"

She was and she wasn't sure if she should be worried or relieved. "Yes, I guess I am. I wouldn't be here if I didn't."

"Not much goes on in this town that Clay doesn't know about." Kate smiled. "Now that you're a little more settled and Daniel seems to be making progress, you could start thinking about what you'd like to do for you. Maybe some work or volunteering. Join the real world and make a life for yourself."

Cassie stared at her as Kate's message sank in. "Here?"

Kate shrugged. "Why not? I did. You can too."

Babs had told her the story of Clay and Kate. "Yes, I get that, but you guys knew each other. You had history here. Everything I know is somewhere else." Would she ever get to go back to her apartment or was that already destroyed?

Adam ran a finger down her arm. "After everything you know about this cartel and what they do, would you really want to go back there?"

She snorted. "My parents would kill me if I attempted to." She smiled at him, seeing the relief in his eyes. "The thing is, I have so much unfinished business there and it really irks me. I'm not the type of person that can walk away and leave a job unfinished."

"I'm the same." Kate laughed. "When I moved here it was under sufferance and it took me some serious thinking time to move passed that and made the decision to stay."

Clay stared at her. "Hang on, wasn't it me that convinced you we belonged together? You stayed because you couldn't resist my charms any longer. Admit it."

Kate nudged him with her elbow. "Don't listen to him. There was no way I could stay until I figured out my future, despite how handsome he is."

Clay clutched his chest as if he was mortally wounded.

Kate ignored him. "What do you need to make you feel more at ease? Maybe I can help?"

"I don't know if anyone can help me to be honest. I have so many cases I was working on and they don't have anyone else to fill in for me. I hate leaving all those poor women without any support."

Kate frowned. "Surely they can call in a replacement for you."

Adam put his arm around the back of her chair, and she felt the warmth on her back. "Getting staff out there is almost impossible. It's the reason I stayed for as long as I did."

"Guilt had you staying?" Adam rubbed her shoulder. "That's not good enough of a reason to stay somewhere that dangerous."

"True but I know I can help them. If I don't, who will?" She shrugged. "The point is, I have commitments I can't fulfill, and I don't like it. That doesn't sit well with me. I have all the time in the world to think about it and it's not a good thing."

Clay shared a glance with his brother and spoke. "I get that. Your work ethic is something to be proud of but in life, there comes a time when what we think we need gets pushed aside for something else. In your case it's safety. I need to do everything I can to protect you, and I will, even if it makes me the bad guy. You have an idea of what we're dealing with here, Cassie. They won't hesitate to slit your throat if it suits them."

Kate reached over and took her hand. "Ever think that things happen for a reason, Cassie? I do. Maybe you're whole purpose for being there was for you to be able to save Daniel, to be there when he needed you."—she gave Cassie's hand a squeeze—"Does that make you feel any better about the whole situation?"

Cassie looked around the table, three sets of eyes stared at her imploringly, Kate's alight with hope. "I give up. You all make sense, and I know I'm being moody for no good reason." She clasped her hands in her lap. "Daniel makes it all worthwhile. I just need to get my head straight and that's on me. Maybe if I had something to take my mind off what I feel I should be doing it might help."

Kate grinned. "I have just the perfect job for you."

***.

Adam watched the excitement in Kate's eyes shine as she laid out her proposal to Cassie.

"What do you think? Are you in?"

Cassie turned and stared at him, her mouth open.

"If you're worried about Daniel, don't be. He has plenty of people at the ranch to keep an eye on him and he's settled down well, don't you think?"

She smiled and some of the tension eased from her shoulders. "Yes, I think he has." She turned back to Kate and held out her hand. "Deal."

Kate grabbed Cassie's hand and shook. "Deal. You start tomorrow if you think Daniel is ready for it. We can discuss your hours and pay rate over a coffee. And if you really need to keep in touch with a few of your clients, you can do it from my office too. I'm not going to be staring over your shoulder so long as the office runs well and the papers come out on time, do what you like."

Adam picked up his beer. "If you start part time, I'm sure Daniel will be fine with it. I'm home and so is Mama. We can all chip in and keep an eye on him."

"I think he is. I also think it's a good idea for me to not be there all the time for him too. That way he will be happier when he starts school. Small transitions and if things go backward, we can rethink things. Daniel still comes first for me, no matter what. Does that work for you, Kate?"

"Perfectly. Congratulations Cassie, Office Manager for the Wishbone Times. You're going to do great."

Clay reached to offer his hand. "Congratulations, Cassie.

If you get worried about your safety at any time, I'm just around the corner."

She gripped Adams hand and blew out a breath. "I can't believe I'm doing this. It was the last thing I expected tonight."

"As I said, things happen for a reason. Tory and I are pretty busy, and if I don't want to work nights, I need someone to do the office side of things for me. It was either I hire someone or leave my handsome hunk alone at night while I caught up."

"I owe you one, Cassie. Kate is far too busy, and I don't see enough of her as it is. We might be able to get out more which will be lovely. We haven't had dinner out for ages, have we, my love?"

Kate leaned into him. "No, we haven't. It was lovely of you two to join us. I miss socializing for the fun of it. Those quiet evening walks with the dogs are a thing of the past too. Maybe we can start them again, Clay."

"Why don't we do a quick walk around town before we go home. You can show Cassie where the newspaper office is, so she knows where to go tomorrow. Maybe point out the easiest way to get to my office just to set her mind at rest too."

Adam agreed. "It's been a long time since I've been in town. Be nice to see it at night."

Clay finished his beer. "How about we give dessert a miss here and pick something up from somewhere else?"

Cassie laughed and the sound went straight to Adams gut.

"I don't think I could fit anything else in."

Adam took her hand as she stood. "Come on little carnivore, let's walk some of that off."

She smiled at him. "I doubt it. I can't remember the last

time I made such a glutton of myself. I'm going to be full for days."

"Not if Mama has anything to do with it." He held her hand as they walked out of the restaurant. "Shame Duke wasn't here to meet you, but they will be home in the next week or so, I think. You can catch up with them then."

Clay and Kate joined them on the sidewalk. "Have you caught up with Ella yet?"

"No. I really must. I've raided her wardrobe and feel a bit guilty over that."

Kate slipped her arm through Cassie's. "Don't. That girl owns more clothes than most department stores and she would be the first one to tell you to take what you need. Her baby has a terrible cold and is miserable at the moment and is struggling to nurse so once that settles down, I'm sure she and Travis will be thrilled to meet you. Right now, they are both exhausted and lacking in the sleep department or they'd have been at the ranch in a shot."

"Sounds good."

Adam held onto her hand as they did a slow walk around town, and he pointed out landmarks and his sister's shop as well as the apartment where Sienna who managed the shop for her, lived with her young boy.

"I went in there first hoping to see Ella before I came out to the ranch." Cassie paused and looked in the window.

"Have you met Ella before?" Adam looked over Cassie's head to his brother.

"No. I read about her and thought maybe she would be a good way to get to the ranch without just walking in and going head-to-head with you."

"You were scared of me?"

She glanced up at him, the shop lights reflecting in her eyes. "Not really but a little bit anxious, I guess. Lissa had said so many things that I just wasn't sure what I was getting into. I thought a buffer might help."

"Fair enough. I'd be interested in what she had to say one day if you're okay sharing it. Not that I need to prove that I'm not the bad guy she probably made me out to be. And I know I probably came off a bit overpowering but under the circumstances…"

She stopped him. "Adam, it's okay. Everything turned out fine. I know you're not the person Lissa talked about. I know that."

Clay broke the moment. "Anyone want churros for dessert?" He pointed at the brightly colored cart on the other side of the street. "I'm having some."

"I'll pass." Adam glanced down at Cassie. She shook her head. "We'll both pass."

Kate grabbed Clay and they ran across the street to place their order.

"I'm sorry, Adam. I didn't mean to put a damper on the evening. It's been lovely and now I've ruined it."

"No, you haven't. I know I can be angry at times, and I'd be scared of me. I was in a bad place when Daniel was taken. I'll be the first to admit that. It was hard not being able to find Daniel and that sucked all the happy from my soul in a way I'll never be able to explain. You were right getting Eli to have your back. I understand that."

She smiled and the relief washed over him. "Thank you." Cassie leaned up to kiss him and he took full advantage of that. He wrapped his arms around her and held her tight against his chest as they explored each other's mouths.

It wasn't until he ran out of air that he pulled back and smiled into her eyes. "I'm so glad you're here, Cassie. Whatever is building between us, it's real for me. I hope I don't scare you off, but we have this reputation in our family."

She blushed, a rueful smile pulling at her lips. "Your mother told me. More than once, actually."

Adam laughed. "Good ole Mama. Between her and Grandpa, don't be surprised if they organize our whole lives. Both of them are terrible busy bodies."

Cassie rested her cheek against his chest. "They're both wonderful, they've made me feel very welcomed into the family already."

"You don't mind them pushing us together?"

She glanced up at him. "No. I thought I might, but I think some of that was me feeling insecure about leaving my job like I did and not being able to do anything about it. When I think logically about my future, I feel like I'm in the right place and I'm good with that."

He scooped her up with one arm under her knees and swung her around, listening to her squeal in delight. The sound making him think of other ways he could make her squeal in delight.

Tonight had turned out way better than he had hoped it would.

19

Cassie arrived at the office at 8:45 am with more nerves than she'd felt on any first day of work. She parked her car and got out, smoothing down the trousers she wore and tucked in the blouse making sure she was neat and tidy. Once she had a chance to settle in at work, she was going to add to her wardrobe. It was lovely that she had clothes to wear but something of her own would make her feel just that little bit more comfortable.

She slipped her handbag over her shoulder and strode to the door, opening it and stepping inside.

A voice came from behind a copy machine. "Be with you in a minute." A few bangs and grunts were followed by a string of cuss words and Cassie bit her tongue.

"Need any help with that?"

A young woman popped her head up. She had a smear of ink on one cheek and a glint of frustration in her eyes. "You can take this to the trash is what you can do." She slammed the paper drawer and stood. "Sorry. It hates me, I swear it does."

The door opened and Kate came rushing in. "Sorry. I got

caught with Mrs. Leigh. She insists I do a story about her incredibly clever cat, and I couldn't get away." She pushed Cassie passed the reception desk and dumped her own briefcase on a desk.

"I guess you've met Tory. Tory meet Cassie, our new office manager."

Tory let out a whoop of joy. "Thank you, Lord." She stepped away from the copy machine and wrapped Cassie in a big hug before pointing at the machine. "That thing is all yours. You're welcome."

"Thanks." Cassie chuckled, eyeing the copy machine dubiously.

"Tory has a problem with machines. They do not like her at all." Kate walked into the little kitchenette and flicked on the coffee machine. "I refuse to let her touch this because she has ruined two so far. No machines for her, okay?"

"Got it." Cassie couldn't keep the smile from her face.

Tory plonked her butt on the desk and grinned. "But I make up for it with my interviewing skills, let me assure you of that. So, Cassie. Where do you hail from? Tell me all."

"Slow down, girl. We want to keep Cassie under wraps as much as possible."

Tory's eyes widened. "Oh, you're the one who ran from the cartel with Adam's son Daniel."

"Yes. That would be me." Even now she still couldn't believe what she'd done.

"Were you scared?" Tory folded her arms and kept her gaze pinned on Cassie.

"I was terrified." And that was downplaying it. She never wanted to feel that unsafe, vulnerable, or scared again.

Tory took the coffee Kate held out. "Thanks. So, Cassie, do you feel safe being out in town instead of hiding at the ranch?"

Kate grimaced. "Sorry, Cassie. This is how she is and there is no stopping her. Probably why she gets so many good stories. Nobody can help but answer when she starts in on them. Tory, go easy, will you? We need Cassie and the last thing we need to do is scare her off before she starts."

"Yes, Boss. Sorry, Cassie."

Cassie took her coffee and pulled out a chair and sat. "That's ok. I'm sure it's a very interesting story to everyone apart from me. Ask away."

"Did it freak you out when you came face to face with that guy?"

She felt she could finally talk about it without hyperventilating. "Adrenaline set in so a lot of it was just automatic. Get out, get away, stay safe kind of thing. Now I'm more settled, I need to keep my brain active and stimulated, so I don't go over it and drive myself insane."

Tory nodded. "Totally understand. If you need anything, shout out. I was born here and know everyone and everything about this place."

"Thanks. Appreciate it."

Kate put her coffee down and smiled. "Right, let me give you a quick rundown of what your chores are and how this place runs."

∽

ADAM KEPT GLANCING at the driveway, desperate to see Cassie drive down in her old beat-up car. She'd been gone all day, and he was more than a little bit anxious to see her. Daniel had been thrilled to get a call from her at lunchtime and once again, Adam was struck by how kind and caring she was. He asked himself for the hundredth time if he was pushing her to be and do something she normally wouldn't, and he didn't like the answer.

"You going to just stand there holding that pitchfork or what?" His father stared at him, a knowing look on his face.

"I'm worried about her, okay?"

His father slapped him on the back and took the fork, digging it into the barrow of hay and tossing it over the fence to the goats. "She's got Kate watching her back and you can guarantee Clay will be all over her safety too. You gotta give the girl room to breathe or she'll second guess staying here, son."

He took off his hat and wiped his arm over his forehead. "I know."

Jack leaned on the pitchfork. "Son, if it's meant to be, it'll all fall into place. Let's not get ahead of ourselves now. Take one day at a time and let her get used to being somewhere new, doing something different. Until we know those men aren't going to come looking for her and Daniel, we're going to be in a holding pattern. Once Clay gives the all clear that they have them in custody and we know what happened to Lissa we can all breathe easy. Romance is easier without the fear of death looking over your shoulder."

"I know, Dad. But sometimes love doesn't wait for things to be perfect, so I'm stuck with worrying about her. Just bear with me, okay?" He glanced over at Daniel, trying his best to use the hay fork the same as Grandpa had done. His son had dogged his footsteps all day, seemingly lost without Cassie there. He struggled to keep his balance and toss the hay at the same time. Adam went over and helped him. "You're doing great, buddy. I need to get you a smaller fork."

He walked back to his father.

"Of course, son. You know your mama and I are right behind you. Cassie is an amazing young woman. What she put herself through for Daniel is nothing less than one of the most heroic things I've ever seen. We love her as much as you do."

A small cloud of dust appeared at the end of the driveway.

"There she is now."

"You can chill out now, Dad." Daniel threw down the fork and started up the driveway.

"Where did that saying come from?" Adam followed him.

Daniel laughed as he ran ahead. "Grandpa. He says to chill out."

20

"How was your day, Cassie?" Babs handed her the bowl of salad and waited with excitement to hear her news.

"It was pretty amazing." She spooned food onto her plate and passed the bowl to Adam who hadn't left her side since she'd gotten home. "So different to what I'm used to in a way, but it still felt like it's what I've always done, if that makes any sense."

Jack smiled and ruffled Daniel's hair. They'd had a great day without her, and it made her even more relaxed because she had been concerned about how he would go without her there as support. The whole family had rallied around to support Daniel, and he was reveling in their love. "I guess you have to be pretty organized for your clients no matter what job you do."

"True. A lot of filing and prep work for Kate kept me busy. I barely had time to worry about anything which was really nice." She sat back in her chair and took a sip of water. "Daniel tells me he had a fabulous time today as well."

Babs laughed. "Felt like old times. He spent more time running between the kitchen and the barn than he used to when he first arrived but he's a growing boy now and needs his food. Plus he wanted to keep his eye on his daddy today."

"And snacks." Daniel giggled and picked at his dinner. "And bottles for the baby cows."

"Calves, son. They were happy to have you around, I can tell you that." Adam nudged Daniel to use his fork instead of his fingers. "Guess you have yourself a full-time job. What do you think?"

Daniel glanced up at his father, his mouth open. "Does that mean I don't have to go to school? I can stay here and work like you do?"

"School soon. Let's get you settled back home first and then we can discuss it." Adam glanced over his head at Cassie, and she blushed. Losing a few months of school wasn't going to hurt Daniel. He was better going once he was calm and settled back home.

"You probably get the scoop on the news, working for Kate." Grandpa scratched his chin, a twinkle in his eyes. "Got any gossip worth talking about?"

Cassie laughed out loud. "Depends if you're interested in the upcoming fourth of July parade or not." She leaned in towards Grandpa, as if she was about to share a huge secret. "Rumor has it this one is going to be better than ever because of Travis. A little bird told me he was going to be on a float promoting home grown beef in Wishbone. Know anything about that?" She raised a brow, a small smirk playing on her lips. "You guys didn't tell me Ella was married to Travis Read, the famous country singer."

"It wasn't exactly a secret." Jack glanced around the table. "He offered to be on the cattleman's float and to do a live performance at the end of the parade. He's one of us now, so when he suggested it, we kind of jumped at it. He loves this town and my daughter, so will do whatever he can to fit in."

Babs put down her fork and dabbed at her lips. "You have to meet them, sugar. I told Ella all about you and she can't wait to come on over. Baby Audrey is settling in well even though she has this terrible cold and she's getting into the routine. Told her there was no hurry because of the," she cleared her throat, "incident, so we will all get together soon. I promise."

"I can't wait to meet them. Travis is one of my favorites." She blushed and shook her head. This wasn't the time to get all flustered over a country music star. It wasn't like she knew that much about him really. Her time alone in the car was spent listening to podcasts. "Not that I had a lot of time to listen to his songs, but the radio station in the office played him a fair bit. Catchy tunes."

Adam nudged her. "He's pretty cool actually. We all like him and he's been the best thing that happened to Ella even if it was a weird marriage to start with. Settled her down and made her realize what was important."

"And she said to tell you that you're welcome to anything in her room. Just like I told you, sugar."

"Thank you, I appreciate it. Now I'm out and about, I was hoping to get some shopping in for my own things. Maybe tomorrow in my lunch break if I can make the time."

"Do you need any money, Cassie?" Adam put his fork down and glanced at her. "I'm not being condescending, but you came away with nothing, so I wondered if it's hurt you financially. I mean, losing everything you owned is pretty traumatic and now you have to replace it and you might want to check with Clay about using credit cards in case they're being monitored."

"No, but thank you. I appreciate the thought and the offer. I might get some new clothes for Daniel as well." She smiled at him across the table. "I have a little cash tucked away so we will be fine."

Babs spoke. "Not necessary, sugar. Toby's clothes that he's grown out of are here and begging to be used. You don't mind wearing them, do you Daniel?"

Daniel shook his head, his mouth full. He plucked at the superman t-shirt he was wearing, and Cassie kicked herself for not noticing that he was in clean clothes every day.

***.

As soon as Daniel's head hit the pillow, he was sound asleep, Adam took Cassie's hand and walked her outside. "Take a walk with me? It's a beautiful night." Cassie smiled, "I'd love to."

They walked toward the front gate, pausing at the fence. A mare with her foal came over to sniff Adam's hand. "Hey pretty girl." The horse extended her neck and sniffed Cassie's hair, making her freeze.

"She won't hurt you. Gypsy is just curious about you and she's not the only one." He leaned back on the fence looking at her, watching the emotions play over her face.

"Tell me about yourself, Cassie. I want to know more about her."

She laughed when Gypsy snorted and moved away, her foal prancing by her side. "Cassie is boring."

Adam rubbed his hand over his jaw. "I somehow doubt that. Why don't we start with your favorite things. Food?"

"Steak and ribs after the other night." She smiled and rubbed her stomach.

"Music?"

"Country. But I tend to prefer listening to podcasts when I get the chance."

"What kind of podcasts?"

She swallowed. Would he be as surprised as his brother? "True crime."

He laughed. "I hear that people who like those are closet psychopaths. Is it true?"

Cassie's turn to laugh. "I guess that's something you'll have to figure out for yourself."

Adam picked a strand of grass and stuck it in the corner of his mouth. "Drink?"

"Water. Plain tap water."

He laughed. "Color?"

"Green. Like that piece of grass in your mouth." Her eyes were drawn to his lips and her hunger to taste him again flared, she swallowed.

"If you could go anywhere in the world for a holiday, where would it be?"

"Oh that's easy, Switzerland. I've always wanted to see the Alps."

"Your idea of a perfect romantic dinner?"

"A picnic basket in a flowering pasture."

His brows raised, a surprised expression crossed his face before a soft smile played on his lips and he reached for her hand. "I think I can arrange that." He tipped his head at the pasture behind them. "The bluebonnets are just poking their heads up now."

"Okay, now it's your turn, Adam? Your favorite food?"

"Steak. Preferably our own."

"Drink?"

"Cold beer."

"Color?"

"Cool blue, like the Texas sky."

"Travel where?"

He smiled. "You know, I've always had the idea to go to Alaska. See the icebergs as big as houses floating by and spend a night watching the great northern lights." She loved that idea. It would be the type of experience you'd remember forever. And she liked the idea of sharing that experience with Adam, too.

"Romantic dinner?"

He took her hands and held them to his chest. "Anywhere you are, is just fine with me." Adam leaned in and placed his lips on hers.

She held her breath, scared to ruin the moment. But when he pressed gently, she opened her lips. Heat raced through her body and she shivered in excitement. Cassie nipped at his lips before he moved and made a trail of kisses across her cheek and down her throat. He stopped when he got to the collar of her shirt.

"Wow." She gave a nervous laugh. "That was some kiss, Adam."

He stared at her with a smile on his face. "Plenty more where that came from. Only if you approve of course."

She chewed her lip, pretending to think it over. "Well, I can't say no to that offer, can I?"

21

"Back soon." Kate hurried out of the office with Tory right behind her, camera in hand to chase down a tip they'd just been notified about.

Cassie opened a search page on the computer and typed in Raoul Estefan's name. She sat back while it all loaded and just seeing his face again made her heart race.

She needed to be proactive and try to find out more about this cartel herself. Maybe working and keeping busy and learning her new role had gone a short way to help her anxiety and bad dreams, but she knew she was just distracting herself. The source of her worry was the feeling of being out of control or unprepared for what could happen. She had to be able to face her fears just in case. That way she could take care of herself and feel a little more in control of her situation if things didn't go the way they hoped. Clay might be willing to stop them infiltrating his town but there was a limit to what he could accomplish.

She tapped the face of her cell and touched the podcast app, opening it up. A new episode was highlighted, and she pressed play, going back to the computer.

After an hour and a half, she was more anxious than ever. The very people she was running from were featured in this week's episode. Cassie felt sick to her stomach. The episode that sent her and Daniel running wasn't mentioned but their past history was. Raoul featured more than any other person. His meteoric climb within the group, the secrecy behind the leader and the way they were spreading into Texas like a spiderweb had her skin crawling.

The people that Raoul had hurt for minor discrepancies were horrific. It appeared as though he took great pleasure in causing pain and destroying families and he didn't try to hide it either. A warning to others.

Something that had always worried her when she worked with her clients. So many of the women she worked with had similar stories. Husbands caught up in the trade and dying for small infringements or in the line of duty. Dealing drugs was a dangerous business and it didn't take much to upset the drug lords.

She shut down the search as Kate burst back through the door. "That was exciting." She dropped her purse on the table and collapsed into a chair.

"What happened?" Cassie slipped her cell into her pocket and tried her best to appear calm.

"Would you believe a traffic accident that turned into a drug bust?" She fanned her face with a sheet of paper. "I've never run so fast in my life."

Cassie paled and took a deep breath. "What? Tell me more." Could this be something to do with 'her' cartel? Clay had spoken of it.

Kate grabbed her hand. "Oh, Cassie, I'm sorry to scare you. No, this has nothing to do with you. At least Clay doesn't think so. Small time stuff. A lady was caught supposedly dealing weed to kids in the park although she denies it. Your cartel is into much more dangerous stuff than that."

Cassie sagged in the chair. As much as she wanted to find out and be proactive, the thought of them being in town already scared the heck out of her.

"That's good then. I wasn't quite ready for that." She gave a nervous laugh. "Phew, thank goodness."

Kate sat up. "You really are rattled, girl. I'm so sorry." She glanced at her watch. "Look, it's almost lunch time. Why don't you head out and do a bit of shopping and take your time. I'm fine here by myself and Tory will be back later this afternoon after she finishes chasing down some other details. Go and enjoy yourself and I'll see you back here about 2 o'clock. Is that okay?"

"Are you sure?" A two-hour lunch break seems a little indulgent.

"Of course, I'm sure. Go!"

Cassie stood, grabbed her handbag out of the drawer and hurried out. It felt as though the office was tainted now she had listened to that podcast there. As though she had brought the evil in and she needed to put some distance between them. Maybe searching for more information on the cartel wasn't what she needed to be doing but sitting there waiting for it to happen around her wasn't in her nature. Cassie was a doer, not a sitter.

***.

Daniel ran down to the barn, his teddy tucked under his arm. Just as he rounded the corner by the wash bay, he tripped and fell flat on his face in a puddle of mud.

Adam raced to his side and picked him up, holding him to his chest.

The wail from his son made his heart ache. "Buddy, it's okay. Let me look at you."

He held Daniel at arms length and checked him over for injuries. When he saw nothing bleeding, he smiled. "I think you're going to live, buddy. No blood."

Daniel held up his muddy hands. "Yuk."

"Yeah, yuk but we can wash that off." He turned to the wash bay and twisted on the tap, rinsing off the mud.

"Teddy." Daniel wriggled out of his father's arms and ran for his stuffed bear. He plucked him from of the puddle and held him out to Adam, his lips wobbling as if he was about to cry.

Adam strode over and took the bear. "You know what, I think Grandma will be able to fix him, good as new. How about we go up and let her wash him while we have some lunch. It won't take long."

Daniel looked up at him with doubt and despair in his eyes and he wished Cassie was here to lay out her logic and soothe the moment. "Promise."

Daniel glanced at his teddy again and then nodded. "Okay."

They walked up to the house together, Daniel clinging to his teddy with one hand and Adams hand with the other.

"Oh dear, what's happened?" Babs crouched down in front of Daniel.

"I fell over and Teddy got muddy."

Babs glanced up at Adam. "I think he needs a bath. How about we do that now?"

"I'll make some lunch so Daniel can wait for him. I promised it would be okay."

Babs took the dirty bear and ruffled Daniel's hair. "I promise he will be fine, honey. Go sit up at the counter and I'll put him in the wash right now." She hurried through the mud room and into the laundry room, Adam followed, turning on the tap over the sink to wash Daniel's hands and get rid of the traces of mud the wash bay hose missed. As soon as Adam dried his hands, Daniel raced over and crouched down and watched his grandmother load the machine.

She added detergent and pushed the buttons and with his little face practically up against the window, Daniel watched his bear tumble around in the machine. "Right, let's do lunch and by the time you're done, so will Ted."

22

The shop assistant who'd introduced herself as Greta, zipped up the dress Cassie was trying on and stepped back, a smile on her face. Cassie stared at herself in the mirror. Peach wasn't really her favorite color, but Greta encouraged her to try it anyway, saying it would look wonderful on her with her coloring.

She was right. It bought out the highlights in her hair and made her skin glow with a warmth that she hadn't seen for ages. She looked happy and healthy.

"What do you think?"

Cassie turned to Greta. "You were right, its perfect." She did another twirl and smiled at her reflection. "I love it." She let Greta unzip her.

When she stepped out of the dress, Greta picked it up and slipped it over her arm. "I have another one that just might suit you too. Give me a second and I'll grab it for you." She ducked out of the cubicle and Cassie held her hand to her chest. She needed this break in the day to get herself calm again. It felt good to do something so normal, like shopping for a pretty dress.

Maybe trawling through the internet trying to find out more about the cartel wasn't such a good idea after all. She thought it would make her feel more in control but it just unsettled her, made her more fearful. From what she'd read, Raoul was deadly, but it was the man he worked for that scared her the most. The so far, unidentified leader was often referred to as The Smoke Lord because he could appear from nowhere and disappear just as fast. The only snippet of information revealed about him in the podcast was that he was from a poor family, but was well-educated. It was said that nuns had taken him in when his parents had been killed and he was very religious. There was no other information found about him...anywhere. No description, no names, not even a rough idea of his age. He was practically a ghost.

It made him more dangerous as far as she was concerned because she could pass him in the street, and she wouldn't know until it was too late. A shiver went over her skin as the curtain was flung open, Cassie rushed to cover herself.

"Here you go. Try this dress on." Greta held up a dusty pink creation that reminded Cassie of summer days and wildflowers.

She held her arms out as Greta slipped it over her head. She smoothed it down over her hips and waited for Greta to do up the tiny button at the back.

"What do you think?" Greta stood to one side, a big smile on her face.

Cassie turned to look at her reflection in the full-length mirror, a surprised smile lifting her lips. She couldn't remember the last time she'd looked so pretty and feminine. The dress had a sweetheart neck and fitted at the waist to fall over her hips in soft folds of silky-smooth fabric. The sprigs of flowers were dotted all over the dress. In her past job, she'd never have worn anything like this. It was way more practical to wear jeans and button up shirts or t-shirts and she'd learned early that wearing dresses or suits could attract unwanted attention—it was a lot better to blend in, in jeans and a comfy tee. It also made her more relatable with the women she worked with and made them feel more at ease, something that was always really important to her.

But she could admit now, she enjoyed dressing up a little. She liked the way the feminine outfit highlighted her curves and the pastel colors complimented her skin tone, making it look bronzed and glowy. She felt...beautiful, desirable.

"I...it's just perfect." It reminded her a little of the clothes she used to wear when she lived at home. Her mother was the consummate shopper and used to shower Cassie with new clothes constantly whether she needed them or not.

Something Cassie missed if she was honest with herself. It was one of the things that struck her when she opened Ella's closet. So many lovely clothes. Just like her wardrobe at home. She'd sighed and told herself what she was doing was important. More important than wearing pretty clothes but so many years of wearing jeans had worn thin. She ran the silky garments through her fingers knowing that they would feel amazing next to her skin compared to what she normally wore. Cassie wondered if she took the job in such a rough town to retaliate against her parents for their overprotectiveness.

Even when she'd left for college it was no surprise to receive weekly food packages, and pretty boxes of clothing because her mother couldn't help herself. Her father had always played it down, called it her mother's addiction. He'd encouraged Cassie to indulge her.

Cassie's friends called her parents behavior overbearing and an inability to let go.

She loved her parents very much but the urge to be independent grew with each year she was away and when she found what she thought was her calling, her parents were horrified at where she chose to go and practice, urging her to work closer to home and not in a drug riddled community were cartels were the law of the land and death was an everyday occurrence.

She'd accepted the job regardless and packed up her clothes and sent them all home much to her mother's dismay. Her eyes went back to her reflection and her mood began to lighten immediately.

"I haven't worn anything this pretty in years." Cassie turned in the mirror and watched the way the ruffled hem floated around her knees.

"I have a pair of sandals that will go with that dress perfectly, if you'd like to try them on." Greta didn't wait for an answer, she ducked out to grab the footwear. Cassie kicked off the slip ons that she'd borrowed from Ella and was waiting barefoot when Greta came back.

"I only have them in two sizes, but I suspect we will be fine." She took the first pair out of the box, unwrapped them from the tissue and handed them over.

Cassie slipped them on her feet and smiled. "Perfect."

Greta clapped her hands. "I knew when I put that dress on display it would take someone special to make it shine the way it deserves. That person is you. It was made for you, I swear."

By the time Cassie headed back to work, she was laden with packages and happier than she'd been in a very long time.

***.

. . .

Adam finished his lunch and pushed his plate away. "Mama, that was amazing as usual."

"Aaamazing." Daniel laughed as he copied his father. He glanced at the laundry room as the machine beeped and Babs smiled.

"I'll go and check while you eat your fruit. Do not get down until you finish, okay?"

Daniel picked up a grape and rolled it around in his fingers. Getting him into healthy eating habits wasn't as hard as Adam had thought. He put it down to his mother's amazing cooking. Not even a small child could resist what she made. "Yes, Grandma."

Adam took a couple of grapes and popped them in his mouth. "How about after lunch, you help me clean out the tack room. It's a bit of a mess and I swear I saw a chicken in there the other day. Before we know what's going on, a flock of babies will make that room their own. We don't need that."

"Adam." Babs called him from the laundry. Her voice was strained and quieter than normal. "Can you give me a hand please."

He ruffled Daniels hair. "Stay and eat everything." He slid from his stool and sauntered into the room. His mother stood by the washing machine, the clean bear in one hand, its stomach stitching open and frayed. In the other hand she held a black velvet pouch.

"What is it, Mama?" He held out his hand for the little bag.

She dropped it into his palm, and he felt the movement as the contents settled against his skin. This is what they were trashing the house for, he was sure of it. If his ex-wife had put their lives in danger for this, he would never forgive her. *Lissa, what have you done?*

"It was in the machine, Adam. Daniel's teddy came apart while it was washing. That must have been in the stomach. Look." She held the bear in her other hand, its stomach stitching frayed showing a gap in the stuffing where the bag had sat.

He knew immediately what was in that pouch could destroy his family and cursed under his breath. "Shit!"

"This is what they were after, isn't it?" Fear shadowed her face and once again, he regretted not realizing Lissa had a drug addiction earlier.

He nodded. "Yeah, I think it might be." He undid the knot and poured some of the contents into his palm. The stones filled his palm, each one a unique size, shape and color. Some flawless white, some with a yellow hue. All were large and magnificent. He wouldn't want to even guess the value of what lay in his hand. Definitely enough to warrant hiding them well, and enough to kill for. He swallowed and poured them back into the bag, tying it firmly before slipping the pouch into his jeans pocket.

"I need to call Clay and let him know."

"Grandma, Daddy."

Adam glanced toward the kitchen where Daniel sat on his stool. "Just a minute." He turned to his mother. "Pretend nothing is going on. His bear got more than dirty, it got ripped and you need to fix it. I'm going into town. Please take care of my son."

"I'll call your daddy to come up to the house and take Daniel, keep him entertained and out of the way."

"Thank you." Adam plastered a smile on his face and followed his mother out of the mudroom. "You're not going to believe what happened to Ted, Daniel. He must have ripped his belly open when y'all landed in the mud. Grandma is going to patch him up for you and I'll be back soon." He kissed his son's head and grabbed his hat.

"But you said we could go down to clean the room for the chickens."

"I did and you still can, but something has come up and I have to go to town. Grandad is coming to help you." He leaned down and looked into his son's face. "Don't let any chickens get one over you, okay? You show them who's boss and if they have a nest hidden in there, I want you to take it back to the hen house. Can you do that for me?"

Daniel nodded. "Back to the hen house." He pushed away his plate, the only piece of fruit left was a raspberry. "That one is yuck."

"You help Grandma fix Ted and I'll be back soon." He strode out the door, giving his mother a thank you glance on the way.

As he walked down the driveway to his truck, he pulled out his phone and called his brother. "Clay, I have something you need to see. I'm on my way into town now."

23

Just as Cassie walked out of the dress shop, her cell rang. She juggled her shopping bags and scrambled in her handbag to find it. "Hello."

"Cassie?"

The voice was familiar. A chill crept up her spine. "Sondra?" Sondra, one of her more challenging cases. Torn between the love for her abusive drug runner husband and the life she faced without him and his money had made her yoyo between the shelter and their house. The last time Cassie had seen her, she had been ready to run back to him yet again. Giving her a business card in case she was needed was the only thing Cassie could do but she never expected a call.

"Yeah, it's me. Listen, um, I don't have much time. Do you...do you think you could come and see me please."

Cassie turned in a circle. "I'm sorry, Sondra, but I'm not in town. I'm in...

"Yeah, I know. Wishbone Creek. Same."

"What?" Her voice was barely audible.

How was that possible? Had she been followed after all

or had they found her? Her heart began to race, and her breathing ramped up, leaving her lightheaded. She started walking toward the office. She had to get off the street. Had to get away from the eyes she swore were watching her.

She bumped into a man, and he reached to steady her. "Woah there, lady. You alright?"

She held the cell in a death grip, only half hearing Sondra on the other end. When she stumbled into the office, she slammed the door shut behind her and pressed herself against the wall.

"Cassie! What's wrong?"

Kate grabbed her, staring into her eyes. "What happened? You're as white as a ghost."

She blinked, clearing her vision. "They...I think, they're here."

Kate squinted. "Who?" She glanced at the cell Cassie was holding and reached for it, holding it to ear. "Hello. Who is this?"

Kate listened while Cassie tried to control her racing heart.

"Okay. I'll let her know." She hung up and dropped Cassie's cell on her desk. "That was a woman you know from the shelter? Apparently, she's the one Clay caught in town with the weed. He's got her in a holding cell. Said she doesn't know anyone but you and wants to see you."

Cassie dropped her bags and put her hands over her chest. "But how did she know I'm here, how did she find me? How?" It didn't make sense unless she had been followed.

Kate gritted her teeth and sighed. "Blame my husband. She overheard him mention your name to his secretary and asked if you were the one and same person she knew. She wants to see you."

"What's she doing here, Kate? Why is Sondra in Wishbone? Do you think it's a coincidence or did she come looking for me?" She pulled out a chair and sat down.

"Maybe it is just a coincidence she's here. Is she a friend of yours Cassie?"

Cassie blew out a breath. "Yeah, kind of, I guess. She's one of my clients. I'm being silly." She smoothed down her hair and tried to smile. "Nothing is going to happen to me, I know that. Clay will protect me." She stood. "I'll be back soon. Don't worry about me." She strode over to the door, gave Kate a quick smile and left.

As she crossed the road toward the Sheriff's office, her mind raced. Was it coincidence? Why was Sondra asking for her help now when she refused her before? Just how many chances did this woman deserve?

***.

Adam got to the end of their driveway when his cell chirped in his pocket. He pulled it out and answered without checking to see who it was. "Hello."

"Adam?"

He slammed his foot down on the break, years of misery came back with that one word. "Lissa?"

She gave a soft laugh. "Yeah, the bad penny surfaces again."

His hand clenched down on the steering wheel. He wanted to rail at her for all she'd done, how she'd put their son in danger, but he was also relieved she was alive, even if just for Daniel's sake. She was an addict so not always responsible for what happened. At least that's what he tried to tell himself. Some days he even believed it. Right now though, he was struggling to have any sympathy for her.

"How could you, Lissa?"

She sighed. "Don't start preaching to me again, Adam.

I've heard it all before. I didn't call for a lecture, okay? I called to make sure Daniel was okay and to warn you."

"Daniel is fine, no thanks to you. How could you put him at risk like that? A cartel, Lissa. For God's sake, a fucking drug cartel!"

Silence met his rampage. Finally, she spoke again. "I know. I honestly didn't know what they were like until it was too late. I was in too deep, you know?"

"Always ready with the excuses, Lissa. Why would I expect anything else."

"I knew Cassie would do the right thing by him. She's one of those people that put themselves on the line for others and she loves Daniel, she'd never let anything happen to him. It's why I called her that day saying I needed to see her. I hope you appreciate how wonderful she is... I didn't until it was almost too late."

"I know how wonderful Cassie is and if she hadn't done what she did, I wouldn't have Daniel back."

Lissa cleared her throat. "Anyway, the reason for my call. I wanted to warn you, Adam."

He snorted. "About the diamonds in Daniel's teddy?"

She gasped.

"Yeah, we found them. I'm just heading into town to hand them over to Clay."

"No, Adam. Don't do it. If they don't get them back, they will come for you. For all of you. Your family will not survive this, I swear on my grave that they will find you."

"Not going to work, Lissa. This ends now."

"No, please Adam. Don't do it. Leave them somewhere and let me know so I can tell them. I don't want to see you hurt." Her voice was fever pitch now, frantic.

"You should have thought about that before you got involved with them."

"You're not listening to me, Adam, they will hurt Daniel, you can't let them."

"I'm not playing this game, Lissa. If I do, this will never end. These guys are going down and if you go with them, that's on you." Her silent, labored breathing echoed down the phone line.

"I'm sorry, Adam. I really am." She hung up.

Adam stared at his cell for the longest time before dropping it on the seat beside him and pulling out onto the road. He would go ahead with his plan and hand the diamonds over to Clay and let him deal with the cartel. All he wanted was a quiet life with his son and Cassie.

But what if she was right and they came for him? Everyone he loved was on this ranch. It would be easier to just hand the diamonds over and be done with it. But something annoyed him about being so compliant. He hated bullies and that was what these guys were. Cassie and Daniel had run in fear for their lives, and he couldn't dismiss that like it never happened.

No, he and Clay needed a plan to stop these guys and keep his family safe once and for all.

He floored it toward town.

24

Cassie clenched her hands as she walked toward the sheriff's office. She was safe. Nobody was going to hurt her in town. This was a safe place. She was fine. She was capable of walking across a couple of streets by herself. She could do this, no problems.

She sensed him a millisecond before he slid his arm under her elbow, before a punishing grip tightened on her arm. "Hello there, sweet Cassie. I've been looking for you. I believe you have something of mine."

Her heart almost stopped, and she glanced at him, her breath caught in her throat. She didn't understand. "Phillip? What are you doing here?" The lawyer who helped out at the shelter? Why is he in Wishbone?

He smiled, his thin black moustache twitching. "Protecting my assets, Cassie. I believe you can help me recover them."

"Your assets? I don't know what you're talking about." Wait, was he here to help Sondra?

He wrenched her to a halt, grip bruising, causing her to flinch. He stared down at her, his dark eyes cruel and very unlike the man she knew who offered part time legal help to the women who needed him the most.

"Don't be stupid, Cassie. I know you better than that. You have my diamonds, and I want them back. Simple." He pushed her again, forcing her to stumble as he walked her down a laneway between two shops to a parking lot. He urged her toward a black truck and slammed her hard against the door, her head hitting the window, sending shooting pain to her temples. She cried out, her hand shooting up to clutch the side of her head. "Why are you doing this? Stop, you're hurting me."

"I will kill you if I don't get what I want."

She tugged her arm, trying to loosen his grip on her, but it was no use. His other hand came up, closing around her throat, as he pushed her back against the truck. His body closing her in. She gritted her teeth and readied herself. No way was she letting this creep hurt her even more.

"I will give you one chance to hand them over and then I start picking off your family members starting with the woman you were talking to just now." He released the hand holding her throat, but his grip on her arm remained solid.

Kate. No way was she going to allow that to happen.

Cassie swallowed down her fear. There was more at stake here than her life. The Wilson family was her family now and she wasn't going to let anyone hurt them.

"I haven't seen your diamonds, Phillip. When I grabbed Daniel, we ran with nothing. Everything he and I own is back in town and I know you've trashed everything." She couldn't keep the bitterness from her voice despite seeing the knife with the curved blade he pulled from a holder on his belt.

"There was nothing at Lissa's house. We searched it." He

lifted the blade, and it caught the light as he raised the tip to under her chin.

Cassie blinked, trying to keep the image of what that blade could do out of her mind. She needed to find a way out of this or she was going to die in this freaking parking lot. She needed a distraction, to get him thinking of something else. In her podcasts, they always talk about getting your attacker to relate to you as a person as the best tactic in life-or-death situations. She needed to get him to trust her. *Think girl, think.* "I don't have what you're looking for, Phillip. I'd give it to you if I did." She kept her voice as calm as she could manage with her heart racing like it was. He lowered the knife a little and it made her a little braver. She kept her breathing steady. "Are you really in charge, Phillip?" She noticed the small twitch in the corner of his left eye. "In the latest podcast about the Mexican cartels, you don't get a mention, but Raoul sure does. It reads as though he is in charge now. Exactly where do you fit in?"

His lip curled into a sneer that made her blood run cold. "You don't know what you're talking about."

"You made fun of me once listening to my crime podcasts." She lifted her chin. "But I've made a point of taking notes when I hear stories about the cartels." She gave a soulless laugh. "Nothing like being fully prepared considering where I work, right?"

He scratched his cheek with the blade. "Your point would be?"

"The leader never stays that way forever. Someone always knocks him off his pedestal. Maybe this is more than you think, Phillip. How do you know the diamonds are all that's missing? Is this just the beginning of the end for you? Are your men lying to you while eroding your profits for their own gain? Just how much longer will you remain in charge?"

He leaned into her face so close, she could count his individual eyelashes. "The child. Where is he?"

"He's not with me."

Without warning, Phillip's hand shot forward, and he slapped her across the face, hard enough to make her ears ring. "I made a special trip down here just to see you Cassie, so stop trying to be smart and be clever instead. I will destroy everything you hold dear if I don't get what I want, the child included."

Sweat began to trickle down her temples, streaming over her heated, stinging cheek. She bit back a whimper when his hand gripped her chin. "I don't have them. I have no idea what you're talking about. Honestly, when I called into see Lissa, I found Daniel on the front step and the house was being trashed by Raoul. When he saw me, I ran. I swear I didn't take anything from the house except the child."

He blinked lazily and stared at her, sending chills down her spine. How could she not see who he was before? He always came across as caring and kind to the women she helped. He'd done so much for Lissa and for...Sondra. *Oh, my god.*

"Sondra. You set her up, didn't you?"

His lip twitched.

"You use the women we help." It all made sense now. Of course, he helped them escape their domestic abuse only to lead them into working for him. He took advantage of them when they were at their most vulnerable. Escaping one hell for another.

"You make them your mules. How could you? Those poor women needed help and you...you abuse their trust and use them for your own gain. You take advantage of them when they have nothing else and get them hooked on drugs so you can control them. You're a monster." She leaned back against the truck, dumbstruck. How could she not have seen what was happening? Did her boss know what really went on down there or was she as clueless as Cassie was?

"I don't force anyone to do anything they don't want. They willingly work for me, and they are compensated well for their efforts." He gave her a cold stare. "But all this chatter isn't helping me get what I want from you, Cassie, is it? My diamonds. Now."

What would it take for him to understand she didn't have them. Cassie shook her head. "If Lissa took them, find her. I have nothing to give you." Her lip curled at the mention of the woman who had put them in this position, but in a way, she's just another one of the cartel's victims.

He laughed. "I have Lissa already and she swears she doesn't have them either. That girl could never hold out on me for long." He smirked at Cassie. "She was rambling something about a child's toy I believe."

Cassie swallowed. Surely not.

∽

CLAY WHISTLED when Adam poured the diamonds onto his desk. "Wow. No wonder they trashed Lissa's house. This must be worth a few million at a guess."

"So what now? I don't want them coming to the ranch for these. Lissa made it clear in her call that they would come looking for them. They need to be made aware that we no longer have them. Can you turn them over to the FBI or something?"

Clay leaned back in his chair, hands over his stomach. "I

can and I will. Last thing we need are these guys in this town." He leaned forward and picked up the phone, pushed a few buttons and waited for someone to answer him.

Adam paced the office as his brother filled in the agent he'd been working with about the latest discovery and discussed how they would proceed with turning the gems over. When he hung up, Adam breathed a sigh of relief.

"Someone will be here tomorrow. In the meantime, they can sit in my safe." He leaned forward, scooped them up and put them back in the bag.

The door opened as he shut the safe door and spun the lock.

Kate burst into the office. "Has Cassie been here?"

"No. Why would she?" Clay shared a glance with Adam.

"That woman you picked up for weed. She called her and asked her to come and visit a couple of hours ago. Apparently she knows Cassie from the refuge. I have this weird sick feeling that something isn't right, Clay. I'm scared."

Clay reached for his wife. "She was fined and released."

"When Clay? When was she fined and released?" Adam turned to look at her. He'd seen this look on Kate before, her mind was puzzling something out. Just like she did with a story.

"She was written up about four hours ago and released."

"And Cassie got the call from her just over two hours ago, so she was probably already out on the street by then. She was the bait, I know it." Kate tapped her nail on her lip as she thought. "They're here, Clay. I can feel it." Kate held out a hand to Adam. "She was scared and didn't feel right when the woman called asking her to come and see her at the jail." Kate closed her eyes and sighed. "I told her nothing was going to happen to her here. What could possibly go wrong walking from my office to the sheriff's office?"

Clay sucked in a breath. "Mom and Daniel, are they safe?"

"I'll call your dad." Kate reached for her cell phone. "Plenty of men and guns out at the ranch to keep them safe. You deal with Cassie and leave home to me."

Clay looked up at Adam. "Call her, please."

Kate put her hand over her cell. "She left her cell in the office. You won't get her." She went back to her call.

Clay was on his feet. "Do you know which way she walked when she left the office, Kate?"

"I'll go." Adam hurried out of the office, ran the quickest route to Kate's office. He went inside and called out. "Cassie. Cassie." He glanced at her desk and picked up her cell. *Darn it. How would they track her now?* Adam hurried back to his brother the only other way she could have gone. Nothing.

Clay was waiting. "Any sign of her?"

Adam shook his head. "Her car is still where she parked it too and her cell was on her desk. We need to send out a search party. If they have her, it's because they know we have the diamonds."

Kate stared at Adam. "What diamonds?"

Clay spoke. "They were stuffed in Daniel's teddy bear."

"No!"

"How the heck are we going to find her?" Adam stared at his brother, willing him to find a solution. "She can't even call us if she needs help." Adam gripped her cell tight in his hand and started to pace.

Clay grabbed it. "No, this is a good thing. We might be able to find her."

"What?" He stopped his pacing and went to his brother's side.

Kate piped up. "Your mom and Daniel are fine. I spoke to your dad, and he has everyone on watch."

"Thanks, Kate." Adam leaned over his shoulder as he opened the cell and scrolled through the apps Cassie had loaded.

"Here we go." He tapped on Find My Devices and opened her Apple Watch. A small red dot pulsed. She was out of town and in the hill country. Someone had her and was on the move.

"Right. Let's get a team together and do this right. We'll only have one chance." He walked to the door. "Russell, we have a hostage situation. Suit up." Russell dropped the pen and pushed back his chair.

Adam scooped up Cassie's cell and followed Clay. "I have my rifle in the car."

Clay stared at him.

"Oh, come on. You know you need my help and I'm not about to do anything stupid with Cassie's life at stake."

Clay poked Adam in the chest. "Fine. Go suit up, but you listen to me, understand?"

"Whatever you say, brother."

Clay opened the comms cupboard and handed Adam a headset. "Turn it on and listen or I'll kick your butt. You're back-up, got it? No heroics."

Adam rolled his eyes but hooked the wire around the back of his head and tapped the earpiece in place. He turned the power on and hooked the control box on his belt. "I told you I would listen. I got it."

Russell threw him a vest and he grabbed it, staring at it in distaste. Cumbersome and annoying.

Clay cleared his throat and glared at him, knowing full well what he wanted to do with it. He slid it on and clipped it in place.

Clay took a rifle from Russell. He held it out to Adam.

"No, thanks." Adam shook his head. "I know my rifle better." He ran outside to his truck. There was no way he was going to lose Cassie now. Especially not to something his ex-wife had orchestrated. Cassie was the best thing that had happened to Adam for a long time, and no way was he letting her be punished for saving his son. He would do whatever it took to save her.

No matter what Clay said.

Clay and Russell followed him and put their weapons in the trunk just as his cell rang.

25

Cassie's panic grew as Phillip drove further and further out of town. The landscape changed from building and street signs, to remote farmhouses and grassy fields. He drove until he found a spot that was off the road and gave him trees and hills for shelter. He turned off the engine and glanced at Cassie. "Time for you to make a call, I think."

She shuddered. Calling anyone was asking for trouble. Did he really think that she believed his promise that he wouldn't hurt her or the family if he got his diamonds back? She knew better. The bad guys never left witnesses. She'd learned that a long time ago. How many podcasts had been made about cartels and their methods.

It made her sick to her stomach to think that all the work she'd done with these poor women had only made them more available to this man. As their lawyer he had unfettered access, and nobody would question anything he said or did. She'd trusted him. They had all trusted him and he'd used that trust to manipulate and deceive. Not a wonder that he could walk among the community and not be noticed.

He wouldn't let her live, that much she knew. The question was how much was she going to suffer before he killed her. She needed to get him what he wanted and then get him away from those she loved without them getting hurt. To do that, she had to stay calm. There wasn't room for her to panic...not yet anyway. Not when Daniel, Adam and the rest of her new family were still at risk.

"I DON'T THINK SO." She stared out the window, trying to slow her breathing before she had a full-on panic attack.

He laughed. "Oh Cassie. I'll give you one guess where Raoul is right now."

She turned her head. He was more organized than she hoped. Was it already too late for everyone now? Was it her fault? She'd bought all of this on them, she had led him right to their doorstep.

He turned in the seat to face her more, glancing in the rear vision mirror. "Despite what you say about being ripped off by my men, I know that will never happen. You see, Cassie, I own them and they will do whatever I ask them to. You want to know why?" He waited for a few seconds and when she didn't answer, he spoke again.

"Every one of my men know that if they cross me, there will be someone else to take their place in an instant and their families will suffer a terrible end. Who do you think keeps their families fed and housed? Who took them in when they were tossed in the street by the authorities with no inclination to take care of them? Who cares about them when the government and everyone else around them doesn't? Me!" He poked himself in the chest.

"What you do at the refuge is a drop in the ocean for what these people really need, Cassie. I'm sure it makes you feel good about yourself, that you're doing something for the poor people in *my* town, but it's just an illusion, little girl. You do nothing compared to what I do for them, what I give them!" He was getting worked up and Cassie clenched her hands to stop herself from shrinking away from him. He was trying to make her feel insignificant, but she knew what she did for the women she worked with. She'd seen the changes they had made together, how those women had found themselves again after years of abuse. And they had helped Cassie grow too. She would not let him take that away from her or the women.

"I may be a drug lord, but I care about my people. More than you will ever know. So again, I ask you,"—he leaned in close, lowering his voice to whisper in her ear—"where do you think Raoul is right now?"

She swallowed the fear in her throat, as he stroked the back of his knuckles down her cheek. A movement behind the truck set her heart racing. A beat-up looking truck filled with men, one leaning out the passenger door staring at her. He had backup. Of course he did. Someone in his position wouldn't be doing this alone. She closed her eyes and tried to slow her breathing.

"That's right. On his way to the ranch. Unless you call and ask for the diamonds to be brought to me, I will let him do whatever he needs to find them. Do you understand?"

She nodded.

He slid his cell from his pocket and held it out to her. "Call someone to bring them here to me. Now. It's the only chance I will give you to stop the bloodshed."

She took his cell and bit her lip. The only number she

knew off by heart was Adams. She'd never imagined this would be the call she would make to him.

Cassie dialed the number and waited, hoping he would pick up a number he didn't know. When he finally did, she almost cried with relief. "Adam...

Phillip grabbed the phone. "Adam. This is Phillip, I'm a... friend of Cassie's. You have something of mine, and I have something of yours. I think we need to talk about a trade. What do you say?"

26

"Cassie, are you okay? Has he hurt you? Where are you?" Adam signaled to Clay as he put his call on speaker.

"Head out of town and take the road toward the lake but go past the turnoff. Take the Willmott Highway and follow it to the crossroads. When you get there, call me back and I'll give you further directions."

"I'm not in the area. I'll be a couple of hours at least." Adam stared at Clay. "Besides, I already handed your diamonds over to the sheriff. He will have to meet you unless you're prepared to wait for me."

"And give you time to set me up? I think not, Adam. Tell him my directions and text me his number." There was a soft chuckle. "Don't try anything heroic Adam. I know you better than you think. Your dear wife has shared how brave and stupid you are. While I admire bravery, it's always stupidity that gets those you love killed." The call ended.

"He wants to do a trade. I don't trust him."

Clay sighed. "Nor do I. This is going to get nasty. I can

feel it. I need to call the FBI in because it's now a hostage situation. At the least they can give us back up."

"They won't get here in time to do any good. This is on us brother. Cassie is in danger now and we can't wait around for backup."

"You're right but I still have to alert them." Clay scratched his jaw, a habit Adam knew he had when he was thinking.

"Do you have the diamonds?" Adam wasn't going to let Cassie die for the sake of a bag of stones.

Clay patted his top pocket hidden under his vest. "Let's go. I'll call it in on the way."

Adam was in his truck first and roared out of town.

"Slow down, brother."

"Bite me." He pulled Cassie's phone from his pocket and stuck it on his holder on the dash. The red dot was still pulsing, but it wasn't moving again. He knew where they were.

Adam tapped the comms and spoke to his brother. "They're at the entrance to the camping ground. I suspect he will take her up to the top of the hiking trial where he will be able to see you coming in."

"Why wouldn't he tell us that from the get-go?" Clay sounded frustrated. "He's setting us up, I know it."

"Because once we're in there, they can block us off."

"Of course they can. He doesn't think he's going to fail then because if shit goes wrong, he cuts himself off as well. No escape for him."

"I can go in from the other side." He mentally ran the track in his mind, wondering if he would make it in time but determined not to fail. There was too much at stake.

"I think we should wait for the FBI. Get a chopper in here and backup and we'd have a better chance at getting her out alive."

"Clay, get real. We don't have a hope in hell of getting them in there undetected. If I go in through the fire trails, nobody will see me or hear me. It's the only shot we have, and you know it."

"Doesn't mean I have to like it."

"You of all people know how this guy works. Do you think he's going to take his diamonds and let Cassie walk away? Or you for that matter? You told me yourself he was an enigma, that nobody knew who he was." His brother was frustrated, Adam got that. But they didn't have the time or recourses to do it any differently. Not if they were going to save Cassie. "This is our only chance of any of us getting out alive."

Clay wasn't ready to give in. "Think for a minute, Adam. He'll be expecting me to go into the camp via the main road. I can have the FBI chopper in and block the exit in case he has someone following us in."

"In the meantime, get your butt in there and hold him off so he doesn't hurt Cassie. I need a clear shot at him."

"You got it."

27

They pulled into the parking lot at the camping grounds and Phillip instructed her to get out of the truck. He stood close to her, the knife in one hand as a deterrent to keep her close by. "Why?" If she was going to die at this man's hand, she deserved to know more about the ins and outs of his cartel.

He took a cigarette from his pocket and lit it, keeping his gaze fixed on her face. When he blew the first lot of smoke out, he spoke. "Why what, *chica*?"

"Why destroy the lives of these women? Don't you think they've suffered enough abuse at the hands of their partners?"

He smoked quietly for a moment, his gaze going around the surrounding area as if scanning for any breach in his security.

Not that Cassie could see anyone, but she knew he wouldn't be alone. If Raoul was near the ranch, the men she saw in the old truck would be blocking the road in here and protecting his back. She knew she had little to no chance of survival so the only way to get through this was to keep her mind active.

"You're rich and white. You will never understand how my people survive no matter how many degrees you have. Think about it. What chance do they have of doing more than surviving in that town? Zero. You know I am correct, Cassie." He squinted as he glanced up at the sun peeking through the trees.

"Crime is our way of life." He shrugged. "I give them what they need. A job, somewhere to stay, hope for the future. I do not let them use my products. That is a deal breaker for me."

"I find that hard to believe." She couldn't imagine a cartel leader having scruples. But then Lissa used his drugs so where did she fit in?

Phillip sneered then dismissed her attitude. "You have never been hungry enough to sell your body or your child, have you? No, I did not think so. You have had everything your little heart desired. I can see it in the way you go about your job. You think you're doing the right thing and giving your time to the poor of my town but in reality, you are only prolonging their suffering. They leave your refuge with no hope for the future, no plan in place to make an honest living to support their children." His voice rose. "I, on the other hand, make sure they have exactly what they need. Just because I deal in illegal drugs, drugs that go to your cities, your educated people, does not mean I do not care about my employees. So no, Cassie. I do not tolerate them using my products."

"A criminal with a conscience. How refreshing." She was past caring if she made him furious. All the years they had worked together, and he had thought of her in this light? It made her angry. "What about Lissa? Where does she fit in all of this?"

"Ah my dear Lissa. Such an enchanting lady that one. She is special to me, even when she doesn't do as I say." He dropped his cigarette and ground the butt out with his crocodile boot before he stared at her again.

His cell rang and he took his time answering it. "Yes." He listened and then gave further directions. When he hung up, he smiled at Cassie. "It looks as though they think your life is worth something, Cassie. My diamonds are on the way."

Her mouth opened. "Why did Lissa have your diamonds? How did she get them?" It had bothered her from the start that Adam's ex-wife would have been able to get her hands on any major assets when she was merely a delivery person.

Phillip laughed. "Dear Lissa. She is such a delight when she is being precocious like that, not something I ever expected when we first got together. We had a disagreement, shall we say. It was her way of getting back at me. Not a clever move but if you knew Lissa as well as I do, you would know she doesn't always think before she acts."

Her mouth dropped open. Phillip and Lissa? Together? Is that what he'd meant when he said she was special to him? She'd never have guessed that in a million years.

"Is she still alive?"

"Why would you care?"

Cassie stared at him, waiting for his answer.

"Si. But for how long is up to her. She is either with me or against me. She cannot have it both ways."

He opened his jacket and withdrew the pistol with his left hand from the halter strapped to his body.

Cassie shrank back against the door of the truck. She

wanted desperately to climb back inside where it would be safer, but Phillip had insisted that she stand out in the open.

"I don't but her son Daniel does. Not that I'll be alive after this to tell him. For my own personal satisfaction, I'd be interested to know what happened to her. I think you owe me that at least since you're not going to let me live. I know who you are."

"True." Phillip checked his pistol and then relaxed, his arm hanging down by his side as if he was used to having everything his own way and wasn't in any danger. "She has been a very naughty girl and I have punished her accordingly. She will not double cross me again, that is guaranteed."

***.

Adam took position on the top of the ridge, giving himself a minute to gather his breath and steady his heartbeat. It'd been a hectic run to get here before Clay arrived at the agreed spot.

He set his rifle up, taking the time to get it perfect. He was only going to get one shot at this. Once his position was exposed, it would be too late.

He glanced through the site and changed the magnification until he got a clear view of Cassie. He held his breath as she stared at the man who had her. He wasn't what Adam imagined when he thought of a drug lord. This man looked like an average office worker. Tidy, nondescript in his clothing apart from the gun in one hand and the knife he was twirling in the other. He glanced at Cassie and sucked in a breath. Her face was flushed, and he noticed a bruise high on her cheek. He checked his anger. That could surface later. That bastard was going down for hurting her.

He turned on his comms. "Eyes on subject."

"Copy, Adam. We're almost there. FBI are sending

backup regardless. Don't do anything until I give the go ahead."

"Copy, Clay." He would do what it took, despite his brother being the one calling the shots. Adam had always been the better shot, ever since they were little kids learning to shoot rabbits with an air rifle. It came more naturally to Adam even though he wasn't the one who wanted to have a career in law enforcement.

A trail of dust appeared above the trees, moving at a casual pace just like they'd agreed. Clay was almost at the meeting spot.

Phillip reached out and grabbed Cassie, pulling her in front of his body.

Adam took a deep breath and counting to ten breathing steadily to focus himself. He couldn't let emotion get in the way or he would lose her. He would have one shot and that was it. Time to put his skills to good use for more than wild dogs that took his cattle.

Clay drove into the clearing just below the rise where Cassie was being held.

"I see you, brother. He is on the ridge above you. Only ammo I can see is a pistol, but he is holding Cassie against his body."

"Copy, Adam."

Both Clay and Russell got out of the vehicle, scanning the area around them.

"No sign of back up for him but they will be there."

"Roger." Clay faced the ridge and shouted. "I'm here."

Phillip pushed Cassie toward the ridge. "Come on up, Sheriff. Make sure you leave your man down at the car."

Adam watched through the site as his brother walked up the path.

"That's far enough." Phillip angled Cassie which made it

harder for him to get a clear shot of the man. It was frustrating that the ridge he was on was facing them, and not behind thm which would have made his shot so much easier. He'd have dropped the man already.

"My diamonds, Sheriff."

"Let her go."

Phillip laughed. "I did not come here to play games, Sheriff. She is of no value to me. I can shoot her on the spot, and you will not get away. My men have come in behind you, so you are trapped, and I will have my diamonds."

Adam touched the button on his comms. "He's lying, Clay. No sign of anyone. They may be out on the main road, but they haven't come in behind you yet."

"I think not. I know these hills way better than you ever will, Phillip. Let Cassie come toward me, and I will hand over your diamonds. The stones mean nothing to me, you can have them, but not before Cassie is in the clear." He pulled the velvet bag from his pocket, showing it off before putting it back. "Cassie, come toward me."

"I give the orders here, not you. She will stay with me until I have the diamonds. Throw them over. Now."

"No. You let her go first and then you get them. You don't have long to make up your mind, Phillip. FBI are on the way, and they really want some special time with you. Now, what's it going to be?"

He lifted his pistol and held it against Cassie's head. Adam bit down his fear and touched his finger to the trigger. The quite whomp whomp of a helicopter sounded behind him. Backup, thank goodness.

"My diamonds or I kill her."

Cassie had her hand at her side, making small waving motions. Was she sending a signal to anyone that might be watching? *Jesus, I think she is!*

Adam hoped that he wasn't imagining it. Her fingers spread wide, as one by one she tucked them into her palm 5...4...3...2...1 and she dropped to the ground. Adam was ready. He shot Phillip as the man raised his pistol to shoot Clay.

He spun around, holding his shoulder and Adam fired again, hitting him in the leg. Phillip went down but as he did, he fired off a wild shot.

Cassie's body jolted, a scream ripped from her throat. She'd been hit.

28

Adam stood beside her bed, holding onto Cassie's hand. The machine beeped with her vitals and an intravenous line fed her nutrients and antibiotics. She was pale and still unconscious, but the nurse had assured him she would wake shortly. The operation to repair her shattered thigh took longer than they thought and just about every member of the Wilson family had made an appearance at the hospital desperate for news.

There was a tap on the door and a nurse popped her head in. "Adam, Cassie's parents are in the waiting room. I suggested they see you before they see her. Clay has arrived too and is talking to them."

"Thanks, Gail."

He leaned down and kissed her cheek. "Back soon, my love."

Adam walked out of the intensive care room and into the patients lounge where his brother was doing his best to answer questions from a very anxious couple. Cassie looked just like her mother.

"Adam, meet Cindy and Ralph Sanders, Cassie's parents. This is my brother Adam."

Cindy threw herself into Adams arms, sobbing. He glanced at her husband and smiled awkwardly. His brother was the one who had the skills to deal with emotional women, not Adam.

"Please forgive me." Cindy stepped back and dabbed at her eyes with a tissue. "I'm ashamed of myself for that outburst."

Ralph put his arm around his wife's shoulders, his face tormented in pain. "We knew something bad would happen one day with our girl working in that place." He sniffed and gave Adam a watery smile. "Your brother tells me you're the one who saved her life."

Adam glanced at Clay. "It was a joint effort. I'm just sorry I didn't do better and save her from the bullet she took."

Clay slapped him on the back. "But we have Phillip and his men in custody now and I think Cassie will agree it was all worth it to shut him down. I'm sorry he hurt her, believe me, but your daughter is one incredibly brave woman, I have a feeling she's going to be happy with this outcome."— pride clear on Clay's face— "The doctors say she will make a full recovery. She needs rest and recuperation."

Cindy opened her mouth. "She can come home with us. I'll take care of her and when she's better, she can decide what she's doing with her future."

Her husband chimed in, and Adams heart dropped. "Not letting her go back there, no matter what she says."

"I want to see my girl." Cindy glanced over at the nurse's station, "Thank you, both of you, for saving our daughter." And then with Ralph by her side, she marched over and asked for directions.

Adam watched them go.

"Don't fret over it, brother. She won't let her folks push her around. Cassie is too strong for that."

A sinking feeling in his stomach gave Adam a bad taste in his mouth. "I failed her."

Clay grabbed him by the shoulders and faced him, nose to nose. "You saved her life, Adam. If you'd taken the headshot, we'd have no chance of shutting them down. If Phillip had been killed, his next in line would have retaliated. God knows what that could have looked like for the ranch or for Cassie's future. Not to mention, he has such a huge organization that it would have been impossible to find everything. Now the FBI have him, they can deal with it all. All we have to think about is getting Cassie back to good health."

∼

CASSIE LICKED her lips and tried to open her eyes. Her throat was parched, and her body felt like a lead weight held her down.

A wave of panic hit her, and she tried to fight her way back to consciousness.

A hand pressed gently on her shoulder. "Cassie, take it easy. You're okay. You're in hospital and safe."

She forced open her eyes and stared up at the nurse who stood beside her.

"There you go, sweetie. Welcome back, Cassie. You've been asleep for a long time. Even I was starting to worry about you."

A shadow moved in the corner of the room and Adam stood at the end of her bed. The streetlight shone on his face.

Tears filled her eyes. "You're okay." She'd been so convinced she would never see Adam again when he hadn't turned up for the diamond drop. Either she would die at Phillip's hand or Raoul would get to him. She couldn't imagine her life ending like that, not when her and Adam had so much future to look forward to.

He moved around to the side of her bed and took her hands, raising them to his lips. "I'm here, babe. Don't cry."

The nurse made a tsk sound. "I don't want you upsetting my patient, Adam. You shouldn't even be in here, you know that. Visiting hours finished long ago. Cassie needs her sleep."

He chuckled. "Come on, Jackie, you know she wants me here. If she asks me to leave, I will but until that happens, I'm staying with my girl." The nurse grinned and smoothed the sheet. "Just take it easy, okay? I don't want her anymore upset than she already is." She walked out giving them privacy.

"Please stay. I don't want you to go." She let out a sob. "I can't help it. He was going to kill me."

"But here you are, alive and ready to kick butt. At least when that leg heals properly you can." Adam smiled. "I'd never let him kill you. We have a future to work out and did I forget to tell you how good I am with a long-range rifle?"

She sniffed as he wiped the tears from her eyes with his thumb. "No."

Adam laughed. "Burns Clay, let me tell you. He's good, but not as good as me which is why I was up on a ridge just above you." He gave a sad laugh before his face turned serious again. "God, sweetheart. I'm so sorry he hurt you. We came in from different directions. I could have gone with a head shot, Cassie but I figured we should get what we could out of him after all he's put this family through. I didn't realize he was left-handed, or I would have taken out that shoulder and he wouldn't have gotten off a shot like he did." He kissed her fingers. "I'm sorry. Last thing I wanted was to see you hurt."

She closed her eyes and sighed. "Adam, it wasn't your fault. It's probably thanks to you that I'm alive. I didn't think I would see another day to be honest." She squeezed his hand. "What happens now?"

"You heal. Let Clay deal with the cartel. You don't need to worry about them anymore." He eased down on the side of her bed, not letting her hand go. "Your mom and dad were here earlier. They want to take you home to recover."

29

When her mom walked in the following morning and saw Cassie sitting up, she squealed and burst into tears.

"Mom, I'm okay." She pulled a face at her father who was close behind and had tears of his own.

"Oh my baby girl. You had us so worried. When Clay called and said you'd been shot, you can imagine how much we panicked." She sat on the edge of the bed and grabbed Cassie's hands, staring at the frame over her leg. "As soon as that comes off, we're taking you home."

Cassie blinked, ready for the onslaught that was her determined mother. "No, Mom."

Her father spoke up. "No point arguing sweetheart. Your mother has made up her mind. We're taking you home so we can look after you."

The thought of having her parents overseeing her recovery wasn't the worst thing she could think of, but it wasn't what she wanted. Her and Adam had discussed it last night when she woke up but he hadn't said he wanted her to stay. She hadn't thought anything of it at the time but now she wondered if it was too much to expect the Wilson's to care for her. Maybe it would be better for her to go back to the city and take things easy. Let everyone heal and move on. She could always get in touch with Adam later. That's if he wanted her to.

God, she would miss him and Daniel. They had all become so close. Like their own little family unit. How would she go not seeing him every day? Who would be there for her when she woke up with nightmares? Was this his way of letting her down gently so he could move on with his life?

Multiple questions raced through her mind at once, leaving her dizzy and confused.

Her mom smoothed down the sheet and tucked it in around her. "Your dad and I knew that no good would come from you working in that place. But you wouldn't listen to us. Had to go do your best which I totally get. Really, I do."

Cassie let her mother ramble on and tried to make appropriate noises at the right time, but she was exhausted even though she'd slept all night. Nightmares had troubled her and with Adam not there to soothe her, she struggled to brush them off and get any restful sleep.

Cassie began to nod off and struggled to keep up with the conversation and her father came to her rescue.

"Poor girl needs her rest, Cindy. We can come back later, sweetheart." He leaned down and kissed her cheek. "Let us know if you need anything, okay?"

"Sure, Daddy. Thank you." She yawned and snuggled down under the blankets as her mother fussed some more.

"Once we get you home, you'll get better sooner. Hospitals are not the place for the sick, I tell you. You get more germs here than anywhere, trust me on this." Her mother kissed her cheek. "I can't wait for you to come home, Cassie. We've missed you so much."

∼

ADAM PAUSED at the door and listened to Cassie's mother chatter about taking her home. His heart aunk. He could hardly blame her when he hadn't come out and asked her to stay last night. Cassie had done more for his family than anyone could ask for. She needed her own family now, especially at a time like this. What a fool he was.

He plastered a smile on his face and stepped into the room. "Morning, y'all."

Cindy grinned at him. "Adam. How lovely to see you. I was just telling Cassie that you heal better at home. As soon as she's ready to be discharged, we're taking our girl home. She needs to rest and recuperate, and I need to spoil my girl. It's been too long."

It was hard to get the words out but for Cassie's sake, he had to sound positive. She'd given him the best gift anyone could, so now he had to make sure she wasn't pressured into staying in Wishbone for him. "I bet you've really missed her too."

Her face lit up when she saw him, and he felt a spark of hope.

"Adam. Hi." She shuffled up against the pillows, wincing in pain. "Ouch, that hurts."

A nurse bustled in. "Time for your meds, Cassie. We need to keep on top of that pain so when we send you home, you have everything under control."

Cindy smiled at everyone in the room. "Any idea when we can take her home? I've missed my girl something terrible. I can't wait to get my hands on her and help her recover."

A flicker of panic raced across her eyes and Adam stared at her, trying to soothe her anxiety while wondering if he should put his heart on the line before she left. Would she come back if she went home, or would she breathe a sigh of relief that it was all over, and she was safe?

The nurse was non-committal as she handed over the medication to Cassie and passed her a glass of water. "That's up to the doctors. You'll have to talk to them later when they do their rounds."

"Come on, Mama. Let Cassie and Adam have some time together. We'll be back this afternoon, sweetheart. Try and get some rest now." He wiggled his fingers and guided his wife from the room.

The look of relief on Cassie's face was priceless. Her whole body seemed to collapse back into the raised back of the hospital bed. "They mean well but Mom is a bit of a handful."

Adam kissed her softly on the lips and then sat down in the chair beside the bed. "I know the feeling. Mama is desperate to come and see you too, but I made her promise not to call in until you say you're up to it."

Cassie grabbed his hand and squeezed it. "I missed you last night."

He took in the dark shadows under her eyes. "Nightmares?"

She swallowed and closed her eyes. "Yeah."

Adam wished he could take away the darkness that lurked in her sleep. "What was it?"

She glanced up at him, worry in her eyes. "They didn't catch Raoul, did they?"

The one regret Adam and Clay had. Did they believe everything Phillip had said? Was Raoul here with him or was he back in Mexico running the business while his boss tracked down Cassie and his diamonds. The only men the FBI'd caught were the few that had tried to trap Clay on the road into the forest.

"No." He ran a finger over her hand, making small circles on her skin. "Is that what happened last night in your nightmares, he came for you?"

She closed her eyes and shuddered. "It was like I was in the house all over again. He was staring at me with his dead eyes, and he smiled, with shiny silver teeth and came for me."

"You're safe here."

"How do you know that, Adam? Is there a cop on my door? Does everyone that comes into the hospital get searched? No. I'm in danger now more than ever." She pulled her hand away. "Now Phillip is in custody, who do you think they're going to come for? Who will they blame?"

"I'll speak to Clay to chase it up. The FBI said they don't think you're in danger anymore but if you're worried, I'll organize something. The staff are aware to immediately report anyone suspicious. If he is around, and we have reason to believe he never left Mexico, we will get him. I promise you that."

"Maybe its best if I go home. I'll be further away and less of a risk to any of you."

Frustration crept up his spine. "Why is it you think you're to blame? Shouldn't they be putting the blame on Lissa because she's the one who stole the diamonds?"

She averted her gaze. "Phillip said something about her. Something about being a naughty girl. I had the impression they were more than just friends."

Adam swallowed the bile that rose up his throat. The girl

he'd met in college would never have fallen for a cartel boss, but he didn't know her as well as he thought all through their marriage. Nothing should surprise him about her now.

"She called to warn me that he was on the way, but it was already too late. I'd found the diamonds and he'd found you." He took her hand again, kissed her fingers and held them tight. "Look, I know this has been hard. When you saved Daniel, you didn't expect any of this. Heck, truth be told, nor did we so I'll understand perfectly if you want to leave and go recuperate at home."

She stared at him. "What do you want me to do, Adam?"

He'd always believed in telling the truth, no matter how hard it was but now he was second guessing that in case it put her in more danger.

Cassie snorted a bitter laugh. "You can tell me, you know. I've survived this far. Whatever you say isn't going to kill me." Her eyes misted and he felt like the biggest heel in the world. He wanted her to stay more than anything, but he wasn't sure it was the best thing for her. He wanted her to love him for himself and not because they were thrown together under the most traumatic circumstances.

"I want us to have a chance to be a family. More than anything I want that but maybe your mom is right. Maybe you need to go home so you can heal and regroup. Make sure that what we have is really what you want."

As soon as he said those words, he could see her deflate into the pillows. She'd already given him more than anyone had a right to ask for. Dare he let her stay when Raoul was still out there somewhere?

30

Adam tucked his son into bed.

"When can I go and see Cassie? I miss her." Daniel's lip wobbled.

"Maybe tomorrow. How does that sound? We can do our jobs in the morning and then I can take you in after lunch. You can pick some flowers out of Grandma's garden and give them to her. I bet she'd love that."

Daniel's eyes widened. "And my special feather I found today. Grandpa said it was from an eagle. I bet Cassie would love that."

Adam's heart melted. His son was so in love with Cassie he didn't know how to break it to him that she would be going home with her parents. Who knew if she would return. Perhaps once she got back to her old life, the idea of being with a divorced man and a child wouldn't be as appealing as she thought it would be.

"I bet she would too. Go to sleep now and tomorrow we'll make it happen." He kissed Daniel and left the room, taking a final peek at his son from the doorway. He left the door open enough to light the room and walked down the hall to his own room.

He felt unsettled. Not just because Cassie would be leaving but something else was bothering him and he didn't know what it was. His mama would say it was the spirits talking to him, but he'd never really given much credibility to the same things she did. Her Creole upbringing was way more colorful than the way Adam saw things.

If he could touch it, it was real. Otherwise, it wasn't true. Ever since Lissa had ruined their marriage with lies and drugs, he'd lost whatever thread of spirituality he had from his mother. Sad and a cold logistical way to look at things, but it was the only way he could protect his heart.

As he showered, he couldn't shake off the feeling. He scrubbed his back with the brush and felt a tingle that wasn't from the bristles.

Darn it! Mama, what the heck was going on?

He finished his shower, dressed and went downstairs. His mother was in the kitchen baking and glanced up when he walked in.

"Going somewhere, Adam?" She had a twinkle in her eyes, noting the hunting knife in its holster on his belt.

"Yeah. I have this gut feeling I can't shake, Mama, and I don't like it."

"Spirits don't waste their energy for no good reason. Go with it and be safe. And give my love to Cassie. I'll go see her tomorrow and take her some decent home baking." She sprinkled dried cranberries over the slice she was making before she slipped it in the oven.

"Keep an eye on Daniel for me please. I'll try not to be too long."

She wiped her hands on her apron. "Take as long as you need. Daniel will be fine, sugar."

He put on his hat and walked out to his truck. All the way to town, he second guessed his actions. How stupid would he look if he rocked up at the hospital and there was nothing wrong. What would Cassie think of his mental state?

He didn't care.

He had to go and make sure she was okay.

They had no reason to believe any of Phillip's men were still hanging around but there was nothing to say there wasn't either. The FBI had him in Dallas so it would make more sense that Raoul was there, looking at ways to free him rather than hanging around a little Texas hill country town to take revenge.

He parked in front of the hospital and made his way up to Cassie's room. The hospital was almost deserted which made it easier for him to spot the outsiders. He walked down the low-lit hallway to the ward she was in, senses on overdrive, scanning every doorway, every nook and cranny for anything out of place. The hairs on the back of his neck were standing to attention and the sick feeling in his gut was growing. Something was terribly wrong, and he just prayed he wasn't too late.

∼

CASSIE WENT to roll over but the cage around her leg stopped her. She groaned. She couldn't wait for it to be gone so she could have more freedom of movement. She wanted to buzz the nurse to help her move so she could sleep better.

It was the cold that hit her first. The feeling of something chilly near her face.

She opened her eyes, her vision adjusting to the dime light and a scream ripped from her throat.

Those dead eyes were inches from hers. When he opened his mouth to smile, the nightlight above her bed glinted on his silver teeth.

"Think you're pretty clever, don't you, *chica*?"

She patted the bed for the buzzer and pressed the button frantically.

He lifted a knife and ran it down her cheek. "You won't be getting any help from her. I have taken steps to give us more time together. Won't that be fun, *chica*?"

Cassie pressed herself back into the bed, desperate to get away from this man but she was trapped by the cage over her leg.

He grabbed her wrists with his free hand and pressed them up against the bedhead as he towered over her. "Phillip sends his condolences and hopes you are recovering well." He snarled and she trembled. The pressure from the knife on her cheek increased and she felt a burning sting. "He has left me in charge while he is, shall we say, unavailable."

His smile made her want to throw up. Evil and cold. This man enjoyed torturing people, that much was obvious.

Cassie tried to keep her voice even, but it shook with fear. "Just kill me and get it over with."

"Now, why would I want to do that?" He held up the knife and she smelled the blood before she saw it on the blade. The pain was instant, and a slow trickle ran down her cheek and neck making her very aware of the damage he had already done. A scream tried to creep up her throat, but the lump of fear stopped any sound.

A siren sounded outside in the distance, and he glanced out the window. "Perhaps we don't have as much time to play as I thought. How disappointing?"

Cassie tried to listen and decide if the siren was from a

police car or an ambulance. Either way, she would be dead before anyone got to her room. She forced out the words. "How did you find us?"

"That was easy, *chica*"—he ran the blunt side of the knife down the center of her chest pushing the blanket down with it, as he continued to talk. She held her breath—"When I searched the house, I found a photo of the child and his father." He shrugged. "Reverse search is incredible, is it not? So much available if you know how to use it." His eyes roamed over her, making her skin crawl. *No, she wouldn't die like this!* She would fight and scream. She would force him to kill her before she let him torture her for his own sick enjoyment.

"Just imagine the fun we could have had if you hadn't run when you did, *chica*. Such a shame our time here is limited but at least I have enough time to take my revenge, no?"

"Please..." Cassie's throat closed over and she squeezed her eyes shut. She didn't want to see when he made the move that would end her life. If this was it, at least she had returned Daniel to Adam, and they were safe.

The blade moved over her chest to her nipple and her eyes flew open. He was so close, she could have spit and hit him in the eye. The evil grin that pulled at his mouth as he ran the knife over her breasts made her want to vomit with fear. Was he going to torture her more before she died? Should she fight and make the end come sooner?

"You made it so easy for our organization to grow, *chica*. All those poor women you set up in town ready for a new life, were like picking ripe peaches. Everything they wanted, we gave them. Money that came faster than they could spend it and in you they had someone who cared for them. I could spare your life for that alone, but I promised Phillip you would pay for what you did." His smile widened showing his shiny teeth. "And pay you will."

Cassie opened her mouth to scream, the lump in her throat no longer as big as her will to go down fighting.

Raoul's body jerked and flew across the room, smacking into the wall. Before Cassie could utter a sound, Adam was on him.

She pressed her buzzer madly, hoping someone would come and help.

Cassie screamed. "He has a knife!"

As if to prove his point, Raoul swung at Adam, missing his face by inches. Adam ducked and swung a fist into Raoul's stomach. As he doubled over, Adam kicked the knife from his hand, and it went skittering under the bed.

Cassie held her hand to her chest as Raoul grabbed Adam's leg and dragged him to the ground, climbing on him. She screamed as he drilled his fist into Adam's face.

"You didn't think your little boyfriend would save you, did you? He's on my list too and so is that stupid kid."

But Adam wasn't finished. He bucked and sent Raoul flying, his head hitting the wall. He slithered down and lay on the floor, stunned.

"Don't threaten the woman I love and my son, you despicable beast." Adam climbed onto him and started beating him with his fists, his punches getting slower with each hit as his energy drained.

After what felt like an eternity, footsteps pounded in the hallway and Clay appeared with Russell behind him as Adam continued to beat on the man sent to harm her.

"Are you okay?"

She nodded, any words stuck in her throat.

Adam dragged Raoul to his feet, pushing him against the

wall and pointed to the knife across the room. "He had that with him."

Russell bent down and picked it up using a glove and dropped it into an evidence bag he pulled from his pocket.

Clay pushed Adam aside, spun Raoul around and slammed him face first against the wall, yanking his arms behind his back and handcuffed him as he read him his rights.

Adam reached over and grabbed Cassie, holding her to his chest. "Are you okay?"

She clung to him, sobs wracking her body.

"Shh, I've got you. I'm not going anywhere, babe. I'll stay right here. I promise."

Cassie sobbed out all the tension and fear that had dogged her since the day she'd saved Daniel. All the emotion flowed out of her like someone had turned on a tap. Now that she'd started, she didn't know how she would stop. Most of it had stayed locked up and only some of it surfaced with her nightmares but was never fully dealt with. She knew better than anyone how that worked but had pushed everything away to help heal Daniel. She wanted to scream and shout and stab Raoul right in the heart after everything she'd been through. But instead, she let Adam hold her tight, rocking her as she cried enough tears to cleanse her soul of all the fear and heartbreak.

After they removed Raoul, and the doctor checked Cassie over. Her leg was fine, but she had a deep cut on her cheek, and a small scratch on her chest. The doctor dealt with her cheek and gave her some pain relief and a sedative to help her sleep, Adam lay next to her on the bed holding her.

"Sleep babe, I'll be here when you wake up. I'm not going anywhere, I promise."

31

"Daddy! Cassie!" Daniel ran into the room and threw himself at his father who reached out to stop him landing on the bed.

"Buddy, hey." He held him close to his chest and hugged him tight. After everything that had happened, he still didn't quite believe his son was home again and needed a pinch me moment more often than not.

Daniel wriggled to get out of his arms and Adam put him down but held onto him. "Be careful with Cassie. Her leg is very sore, so we need to look after her."

Daniel nodded then walked around to the other side of the bed and leaned in gently to take her hand. "I missed you."

Tears filled her eyes, and she shared a glance with Adam that made his heart race. "I missed you too, honey. But I'll be home in a few days."

Mama stood at the door taking in the scene. "Well, that's good news, sugar. I bought you some food because I know what these places are like." She bustled in and put a large, insulated bag on the chair near the bed. "They try to give you nourishing meals, but you can't beat homemade." She unzipped the bag and took out a container, putting it on Cassie's tray. "I thought you might like some of my chili for lunch. There's enough for both of you, so don't you go looking at me like I've forgotten you, Adam."

She pulled out a small bag with cutlery and serviettes and put it beside the container and then produced a couple of brightly colored bowls and a serving spoon. "Help yourselves now. Don't worry about Daniel and me. We ate, didn't we, sugar?"

"Yes, Grandma. And we had cookies." He held three fingers up.

"Three?" Adam tried to look horrified but came off lame instead. "Mama, really?"

Mama batted her hand at him. "Oh, stop it, son. What harm can it do? He had fruit as well so you can calm right down. Eat now."

She pulled a plastic container of fruit out of her bag and removed the lid, leaving that on the table and then sat down. "I had a call with Clay early this morning, so we don't need to discuss any of that right now. Tell us what the doctor said about your leg, sugar. When is he letting you come home?"

Adam made a plate of chili for Cassie and pulled the table closer for her. She took the bowl with a smile that made him warm all over and Mama didn't miss the look either.

Cassie was still feeling a little bit shaken after last night but had insisted on discussing their future when she woke up early this morning. They lay in bed together and watched the dawn break as they spoke with their hearts about what they wanted.

"I have physio today. If I can get around on crutches well

enough, he will let me leave. It's going to be a long recovery though and I don't want to be a burden to you or the family."

His mother glanced at him, a question in her eyes seconds before she spoke. "Sugar, you're family now. That's no burden at all. Tell her, Adam."

He sat beside Cassie. "I told her Mama, but she insisted on running it past y'all anyway."

A sob came from Daniel. "You promised." He threw himself at his grandmother, wailing into her chest.

Adam got off the bed and picked up his son. "Buddy, hey, listen to me."

Daniel continued to cry, his little body shaking with it, he couldn't console him.

Cassie spoke gently. "Adam, put him down here." She put her bowl on the table and pushed it away leaving room for Daniel.

***.

Adam put Daniel down on the bed next to her and Cassie pulled him in against her body, wrapping her arms around him. It took him a few minutes to settle, but once he did he sniffled and then glanced up at her. "You p-prom-promised." His little broken words tore at her heart.

"I did. And I don't want to leave you, Daniel. I always want to be close to you, sweetie. But my leg is sick and because it's so sick it will need lots of time and medicine and doctors to make it better. That means I won't be able to walk around or play or drive for a while." He frowned at the news she wouldn't be able to play so she knew he was following what she was saying. "That means someone has to take care of me all the time because I won't be able to do everything for myself. That's a very big burden to put on someone, sweetheart." She cupped his face in her hand, stroking his cheek with her thumb. "My mom wants me to go home so she can take care of me."

He glanced at his father and grandmother before looking up at Cassie again. "I can look after you." He wiped a hand across his face, smoothing out the tears as his eyes brightened with hope. "You looked after me, didn't you?" He nodded his head encouraging her answer.

"Yes, I did but that's different. You needed me."

He grabbed her hand. "You need me. I can do it. I know I can. I'm a big boy now, Daddy told me I am." He stared at her with his heart in his eyes and she wanted to cry with the emotion of it all. She was so in love with this little boy. There was one problem though.

"But what about my mom? What am I going to tell her?"

Daniel shrugged. "I need you more than she does."

"Well....."

"Please, Cassie. Please stay. We all need you. And if she misses you or gets sad, she can just come and visit us. I can look after her too." He puffed out his chest and her heart swelled. He was so darned adorable.

"She can have a sleepover in my room, and you can sleep in Daddy's room."

Adam pressed his lips together but the glint in his eyes was enough to know how much he appreciated that idea.

Daniel glanced at his father. "Dad. Tell her."

Adam ruffled his son's hair. "I told her this morning, buddy. She wanted to talk to you first though."

Daniel's mouth opened and he stared at them both.

"Does this mean what I think it means?" Mama was on her feet, her face lit up with the biggest smile.

"Yes, Mama. Cassie is staying and we're officially a couple. We just have to tell her parents and I don't know how they're going to take it. They were looking forward to having time with her while she healed."

Mama waved her hand. "Easy fix. We take Daniel's advice, and they can come and stay at the ranch. Lord knows we have way too many empty rooms anyway." She moved to Cassie and wrapped her in a hug. "Sugar, I'm so glad. You three belong together."

"We do, Mama. That we do." He grabbed his bowl. "I'm starving. Clay is going to be coming over later this afternoon for a statement and hopefully that's the end of it all. The physio is going to give Cassie a workout, so I want to be here for that, then I'll come home. Hopefully not alone too."

Mama shook her head. "You stay here with Cassie. Grandpa is coming in later and can bring you some clean clothes. I think she'd appreciate you being here to soothe her and help with the physio, right, sugar?"

Cassie nodded. The last thing she wanted to face was being on her own right now. Even though Raoul had been taken away, she was still fearful Phillip would send someone else to do what he couldn't. After Phillips deception and manipulation, she had lost all trust in the system to protect her, and Adam was the only one who made her feel safe.

"I can stay." Daniel looked imploringly at his grandmother.

"Young man, you have chores to do at the ranch. Grandpa said you could have this time off to visit Cassie, but you had to go and finish up, remember? Those baby chicks aren't going to feed themselves."

Daniel dropped his head. "Yes, ma'am."

"Grandpa can't come and visit if you aren't there to take care of your orphans. Fair is fair now."

He stared at his father, his tiny brows pulled together in a serious expression. "We made a deal, Dad. And a man has to keep his promise, so guess you get to look after Cassie." Adam smirked, trying to hold back a laugh.

"Thanks son. You can do your fair share when she comes home, I promise."

Chatter came their way and Cassie froze. "Mom and Dad. This is going to be fun."

Daniel stood straight. "Don't worry, Cassie. I'll look after you *and* your mama. We have a deal, right?"

Cassie smiled. "We do, Daniel." And it felt good to belong. She just had to explain it to her parents but with the Wilsons helping her, she didn't think it was going to be too hard to deal with. In fact, she's pretty sure it wouldn't take Daniel much time at all to have both her parents wrapped snuggly around his adorable little finger.

The End

Milton Keynes UK
Ingram Content Group UK Ltd.
UKHW030855111124
451035UK00001B/47